Devoted Heart

A Modern Nativity

Bill Myers

Published by Amaris Media International in conjunction with Stonewater.

Cover Design: Angela Hunt

Photo copyright jfk image

Another one for Brenda:
Whose patience, as I keep learning to become a better husband and friend, always amazes me.

INTRODUCTION

Over the years, I've received hundreds of letters on how my novel, "Eli" (a retelling of the Gospel as if it happened today), has changed lives. Some folks claim they make a point to read it once a year, pastors say they preach from it, schools make it required reading. And my favorite e-mails are the ones that say, "I've been a Christian all my life and now I finally get it."

"Getting it." That's why I wrote "Eli"—so that readers (myself included) could see Jesus as a living, breathing person, not some distant, historical figure or religious painting. By stripping away the religious varnish we've encased Jesus in and putting him in a 21st century world like our own, it sets Him in front of us. It removes the 2,000 years of history we may use to insulate ourselves from the real person, and puts us face to face, with who He really is.

That's the same reason I've written, "Devoted Heart." I wanted to take Joseph and Mary out of the glittery Christmas cards and to experience what they must have really gone through. I wanted to explore their emotions, their faith, their fears, and their doubts. I wanted to feel what it must have been like to be a young couple given such an astonishing call and who set out to fulfill it despite the odds. Is the book accurate? Hardly. I've probably missed the point dozens of times. But if it only captures a fraction of what they went through, if it helps put just a little flesh and blood on the sterile statues and cut-out manger scenes then, at least for me, it's been a success.

As with "Eli," this writing doesn't hold a candle to the real accounts found in Scripture. And if you haven't read them for a while, don't waste your time here. The Word of God is infinitely superior to the prayerful imaginings of one man. Also, since I'm in a confessionary mood, let me point out another failure—having to ignore the rich Jewish history that was so important for the real Joseph and Mary. There are many great writers who, over the centuries, have captured that. My purpose was to simply explore the couple's heart. And if this book can do just a little of that, if it can help us appreciate just a little more deeply what these great heroes of faith may have actually experienced, then it's served its purpose. That's what the writing did for me. And what I hope the reading will do for you.

Thanks again for taking another journey with me,
Bill
www.billmyers.com

ONE

All right, Joey. Taxi's here."

I looked up to see Leroy Burton's big blurry form come around the bar. We graduated the same year. Played football and basketball together since middle school. Far as I know, we were in the same kindergarten. Town is that small.

I motioned to my glass. "One more for the road."

"No, you've had enough *one mores* for the night."

"What time is it?" I looked at my watch but couldn't seem to see the numbers.

"Time for all good war heroes to call it a day."

"Don't call me that. I hate it when people call me that." He disappeared behind me. "Where'd you go? Where'd you-- There you are. Do you know who the real heroes are? Do you?"

"No," he said, holding up my coat. "Why don't you tell–"

"I'll tell you. Men and women who lost their lives. Who lost arms and legs, those are the real heroes."

"No argument there."

"How many arms do you see, huh? How many legs?"

"'Bout the right number of each, I'd say."

"Exactly."

He held out a coat sleeve for me. "Let's go."

It took a couple tries to find it. "It was my fault. I should have known better."

"What?"

"Mary. Mary! Are we or are we not talking about Mary?"

"If you say so."

We should have got married before I left."

"Come on, man. It's Mary McDermott. Who would have thought?"

"We were engaged."

"And you were out of country eleven months."

"We were going to get married."

He helped my arm into the other sleeve. "It's a new world out there, Joey. If guys don't make the move on chicks by the second date they think he's gay."

"It's Mary. We were engaged."

"So, I hear."

"You heard? Does everybody know?"

"That you were engaged?"

"No."

"Sorry?"

"Why didn't you tell me? Why didn't *somebody* tell me?"

"They shipped her off to some relative before anybody knew. She's only been back a few weeks." He slipped his shoulder under my arm.

"Pastor McDermott's kid. Mr. straight-as-an-arrow, stuffy-butt McDermott."

"And up we go." He helped me to my feet. Not that I needed it. I could walk just fine, soon as the floor quit moving.

"It was Johnson, wasn't it?" We started toward the door. "Todd Johnson always had a thing for her."

"We all had a thing for her, Joey."

"All of you?"

"Not that way. She's everybody's kid sister, you know that. We all love Mary."

"Sixteen months and we never even made out." Leroy opened the door and we stepped into the cold, December rain. "Sixteen months! She said, 'I want to save myself for our wedding night. I want it to be my gift to you.' And I believed her!" I tilted back my head and shouted into the rain, "I believed her!"

Leroy opened the car door.

"I'm gonna kill him."

"Who?"

"Tomorrow morning I'm gonna go right up to his door, knock real politely, and when he opens it I'm gonna kill that son of a–"

"And in you go." Leroy dumped me into the back seat.

"Hey there," the driver said, "it's the war hero."

I would have called him out on it. Maybe I did. I don't remember. I barely remember getting into the cab. And I sure don't remember getting out.

But I remember the dream . . .

TWO

I know what a dream is and, actually, this was no dream. All right, maybe I was asleep, but it was more real than anything I could have come up with . . . asleep or awake. At first the pieces were sketchy and fritzy, which is the part I'll take responsibility for. Me and Johnny Walker, which for the record, was only the second time I'd ever been drunk. The first was a stupid high school thing, which I'm not proud of either.

Anyway, I was in a circus tent, dressed up like a clown, complete with a big painted grin, those giant floppy feet, and a red rubber ball for a nose. Everybody was laughing—my old teachers, Coach Morrison, Mom, Dad, buddies from high school, even Charlie Riordan from my outfit. Always Charlie Riordan. Everyone sat on the bleachers yucking it up as Todd Johnson smashed a banana cream pie into my face . . . and then another . . . and another. It was all a big, gigantic joke with me as the punch line. And no, Dr. Freud, I don't need anyone to explain the symbolism to me.

But then things got interesting. At first I heard the voice—faint, rumbling like distant thunder:

"Joseph . . ."

I paid no attention. I was too busy chasing Todd around in one of those little clown cars. When I finally got him cornered, I unfolded myself from the car, leaped out, and pulled a giant confetti gun on him. He dropped to his knees, whimpering like a baby, as I prepared to fire. Then I heard it again. Louder:

"Joseph . . ."

I looked all over but saw nothing. Except the whole audience looking up. I followed their gaze just in time to see a trapeze artist, dressed in brilliant, white light. He missed his trapeze and the crowd gasped as he started to fall.

But he really didn't fall. He floated. Toward me. And the closer he got, the brighter his light grew until he was blazing, as bright as the sun, maybe brighter. The crowd disappeared. So did the circus. I was somewhere else. Some place so still, so silent I could only hear my breathing . . . and the voice that was so loud it thundered like a waterfall.

"Joseph . . ."

I've been afraid before. You don't get caught in a firefight without experiencing a little fear. But this was colder, more gut-clenching than anything I'd ever felt. So terrifying I couldn't move. And the light. Intense. Piercing. His face, what I could see of it, glowed and shimmered with the light. Maybe it was the light. One thing I can tell you, as I looked on, it stopped being the face of a man. It glimmered and morphed until it became the face of an ox.

I shut my eyes and reopened them. Now it was the face of an eagle.

"Joseph, son of David . . ."

The face flickered and changed again. Into the face of a lion. Then one last flicker and it was a man's again. As I stared, giant wings unfurled behind him. Ten, fifteen feet across. They pulsed and shimmered with the same light as the face.

I felt my legs turn to rubber, which was okay since now was as good a time as any to drop to my knees. That was the only response a person could have in the presence of so much . . . well, there was no other word for it but what you religious types call . . . "glory." It was so powerful I could no longer keep looking. I lowered my head, staring at the ground. The voice continued to roar. It wasn't angry and it wasn't yelling. Just roaring. Exploding with power.

"Do not be afraid to take Mary home as your wife."

I scowled, trying to keep my head clear, trying to keep from passing out.

"What is conceived in her is from the Holy Spirit."

The voice came from all around me. And inside. It was like every cell in my brain, in my whole body, vibrated with it.

"She will give birth to a son and you are to give him the name Jesus because he will save his people from their sins."

He paused. I took a ragged breath and braced for more. But that was it. Nothing more except the terror and glory . . . which started to fade, along with the light. I took another breath, and then another. Finally, I found the courage to lift my head.

And he was gone.

No goodbyes. Nothing. One minute I was surrounded by blinding light and paralyzed with fear, the next I was lying in bed, catching my breath, and staring at the ceiling.

When I could move, I rolled over and looked at the alarm. It glowed crimson, 2:54. I lay there another minute. Maybe two. When I was sure going back to sleep was impossible I rolled out of bed and padded down the worn, carpeted stairs. Once in the kitchen, I threw a mug of instant coffee into the microwave. The dream was over, but the words lingered.

"Take Mary home as your wife."

The rest made no sense, but I got that part. I pulled out a kitchen chair and sat. My mind was clear. No headache and no payback with a hangover that should have been my due.

Just the words.

THREE

The sun was just peeking over the neighbor's frost-coated roof when Mom joined me on my third cup of coffee. She wore that same pink, terrycloth robe she'd had since before I left. New slippers. Same brand as always, but new. That was Mom. Once she found something she liked, she kept it. Could explain why she and Dad were going on their 34th year. Not that they didn't have their moments. Both were as stubborn as mules. But their parents had been farmers. And their parents before them. So their no-nonsense outlook—you can't fool the earth, so don't try to fool me — always won out. They'd made a commitment and despite the fights, and threats, and once or twice, a flying utensil, they were sticking together no matter what.

Which explains her response when I told her my plan.

"You're not serious?" she said.

"Sure, why not?" I tried sounding like it was no big deal. "We go someplace out of the way, have a little civil ceremony, come back and set up house. Tongues will wag for a while, but eventually no one will even–"

"After what she's done? The way she's treated you?"

I took a sip of coffee.

"And the embarrassment? Not just to you. The jokes they're telling down at the mill. Your father, he didn't say much, but I heard from some of the others. . ." She hesitated.

"What, Mom? What did you hear?"

"One of the younger guys, you know how they're always shooting their mouths off."

"What'd he say?"

"Some kid made a crack to your father. I'm not exactly sure what, but . . . well, your father and him, they kinda got into it."

"Dad?"

"They put him on a week's leave without pay."

"What?"

She glanced down at her coffee—embarrassed, but you could also hear a little of that working-class pride. "Guess he busted the kid's nose up pretty bad."

I still couldn't believe my ears. "Dad?"

She looked out the window. "'Course, old man McDermott, he just keeps on preaching like nothing's happened. All holier than Thou. I tell you, I never did like that family, putting on airs and acting like—"

"The McDermott's don't put on airs."

"What do you call it when he stands behind a pulpit every Sunday telling people they're not good enough? That they have to be all holy and perfect?"

"He's always done right by me," I said. "A little overprotective with his daughter, but he's a good guy."

"Maybe he is, maybe he isn't."

"Meaning?"

"The apple never falls far from the tree."

I stared at her.

"Don't look at me that way. Besides, you know what they say about preacher kids."

"Mom. It's Mary McDermott."

She stared back out the window, doing her best to bite her tongue. But her feelings were clear. Her silence judge, jury and verdict.

And she was right. So why was I defending Mary? Don't get me wrong, last night's guest appearance with all its special effects, definitely made an impression. But I was still mad. Big time. And humiliated. And betrayed. And . . . well, the list goes on.

But I knew her. I knew Mary McDermott. At least I thought I did. She was the girl I teased throughout elementary school. In middle school, she was the one I always made a mental note of if she was nearby. And in high school, she was the one I became best friends with. We were always there for each other. When she couldn't wrap her head around Chemistry or lost the election for student body president, I was there. When I got hospitalized with a minor concussion or when Cindy Prescott dumped me and I had no one to ask to Homecoming, she was there. She never told me how many guys she turned down waiting for me to ask, but she was there.

That was Mary McDermott. Sensitive, thoughtful . . . and pregnant with somebody else's kid! My gut tightened. My thoughts more than a little scrambled.

Mom cleared her throat. "Want some breakfast?"

"Not if it's trouble."

"Nonsense. Your father's getting up in a few minutes anyway, so—"

She was interrupted by the doorbell. We traded looks.

"Who could it be this time of morning?" she said.

I started to get up to answer it.

"Sit, sit," she said. "Finish your coffee." She rose and ambled out of the kitchen.

My mind went back to Mary McDermott . . . the girl who always passed on seeing raunchy movies. The looker who knew how to dress, but never used it to show off her body. Everybody's friend, but who never joined in the drinking, drugs, or even bad language.

And she couldn't wait a year! Eleven months?

This was the down-to-earth beauty I wouldn't dream of making moves on. Oh, I'd dream, but I wouldn't dare. And she does it with some other guy? My jaw clenched. Whoever it was, I'd find him. I swear to God, I'd find him and–

"What is conceived in her is from the Holy Spirit."

The words made no sense. And if they were supposed to make things easier, forget it. Seriously, did she have any idea how many women I could have had? Like Leroy said, it's a new world out there. And I'm a good-looking guy. There were opportunities. Lots of 'em. But I turned them down. Why? Because I loved her. I had my chances, but I honored her. Honor! A word she'd obviously forgotten.

"Joey, can you come here a minute?"

I scooted back my chair, rose and wandered into the living room, my mind still racing. And what does she do? She can't wait to hop into the sack. With who? Johnson? Maybe. Maybe some other sweet talking guy. Or guys. Like Leroy says, they were waiting in line. And now I'm the joke. The guy with pie all over his face. The guy whose old man gets into a fight at . . . I slowed to a stop.

There, in the doorway, silhouetted by the morning light, stood Pastor McDermott. Balding, early fifties, in an overcoat and suit. Always a suit. And beside him . . . Mary. She was bundled up in a blue ski jacket, white scarf and mittens. The sun flared behind her, making her hair glow. For a moment I forgot to breathe.

She never looked up, just kept staring down at her mittens. I had no idea what to say. Her dad saved me the trouble. "Joseph."

I nodded. The muscles in my jaw were getting a work out but I didn't answer. Didn't trust my voice. My nails dug into my palms, but I didn't speak. Only stare. At her. Slender, five four, and even more breathtaking than I remembered. I'd waited eleven months for this moment.

Thought of it every day. Dreamed it every night. And now I couldn't speak.

After what seemed forever, she raised her slate blue eyes. They were red and swollen.

My throat tightened.

"Do not be afraid to take Mary home as your wife."

I took a slow, steady breath.

Her eyes faltered, then looked back down. I caught the reflection of a tear tracking down her cheek.

Mom cleared her throat. "Would you like to come in?"

McDermott looked to his daughter. She gave no answer.

"What is conceived in her is from the Holy Spirit."

I scowled at the words but they kept coming.

"Take Mary home . . ."

I swallowed.

". . . as your wife."

I took another breath. My own eyes burned with moisture but I couldn't look away. And then, having minds of their own, I felt my fists unclench, my palms turning toward her. Not my arms, they still hung frozen. Just my hands. I opened my mouth. Words still wouldn't come. They didn't have to. She saw what was going on, read my mind as she always does.

And she raced to me.

Before I could stop myself, I was holding her. I felt her hot tears against my neck, her body trembling. Was I still angry? Yes. A thousand times over. But even as I held her, tears spilled onto my own face, running down, mixing with hers.

Finally, I forced the word from my clogged throat. It came, but barely a whisper. "Mary . . ." I pulled her closer, buried my face into her hair. "My Mary."

FOUR

She motioned to my coffee. "You quit using milk?"

"I lost the taste."

"Take yours like a real man?" It was supposed to be a tease but it fell flat.

We just kept sitting there, redefining the term, awkward. I was never good at putting my thoughts into words, they always came out stupid and clumsy. Not like Mary. And now with everything so jumbled up in my head I wasn't even sure where to start.

Mom and old man McDermott had the good sense to let us get off by ourselves. Though it took an extra nod from Mary to her dad, like she was telling him I could be trusted.

Like *I* was the one with trust issues.

We'd retrieved my beater pickup from the back of Leroy's Bar and Grill, and after a little coaxing, I got the engine to fire up in the cold. The heater wasn't so cooperative, leaving the cab freezing. It had never been a problem for us before — the joy of bench seats—but now Mary stayed on her side, miles away. It was the right choice. I don't know what I would have done if she tried scooting next to me.

It was the right choice, but it broke my heart.

When we got to the town's one and only Starbuck's—or as Mary calls it, "St. Arbucks"—I parked and crossed around to pry open her door. I helped her down and offered my arm so she wouldn't slip on the ice. Besides the little living room scene, it was the first time we'd touched. It felt good and awful.

After ordering, I took her coat and paused only a second at the size of her belly. We found a table at the far end of the room. I took a seat with my back to the wall so I could keep an eye on things. Survival technique. I was back home, but old habits die hard.

Knowing where I sat and why, Mary started up the conversation again. "Was it hard for you?"

I looked at her.

"I mean I got your e-mails. About Charlie. But I could tell you were leaving out a lot of—"

"It was hard for everybody." My voice was sharper than I wanted. I looked out the window.

She nodded, then softly added, "But at least you came home."

I tried not to scoff, but like I said she had a way of knowing what I was thinking.

We sat there in the silence. Her ring, the one with the little diamond I gave her nearly a year ago, sparkled a moment in the sunlight. She saw me see it but said nothing. I guess she figured it was my turn.

I swallowed, looked out the window. "So . . . when's it due?"

She waited until I turned to her. "It's not an it. It's a he."

"You've done the tests?"

She shook her head.

"Then how do you—"

"I just know."

I looked down at my coffee, then up and across the room just in time to see a gray-haired couple glance away.

I'd seen them before, off and on, whenever Mary dragged me to her father's church.

Alright. Enough moping. It was time to suck it up and cut to the chase. I turned back to her and said, "Whose?"

Her eyes faltered ever so slightly, but she held my gaze.

"Whose?" I repeated.

She answered, her voice soft but steady. "You know in the Bible, all those prophecies talking about a great leader that's going to come?"

My jaw tightened. This was not the time for her to get religious on me.

"In Isaiah 7:14 it says—"

"I'm not in the mood for a Bible study!" I was way too loud and way too angry. And we both knew it.

She looked at me a moment, then nodded and sat back in her chair. "No . . . you're not."

A shattering explosion came from behind the counter. I jumped, my body on full alert . . . until I saw one of the employees had simply dropped a mug.

"Sorry," he said to no one in particular.

I took a breath and then another. I turned back to Mary, her eyes on me the whole time. I saw the concern but wasn't going to have it. "So that's it?" I said. "That's all you're going to say for yourself?"

Her answer was still soft, but had that quiet strength she was known for. "That's all you can hear." More gently, she added, "For now."

"What's that supposed to mean?"

She shook her head.

I pressed in. "What's throwing the Bible at me got to do with anything?"

"I wasn't—" She caught herself and simply shook her head.

"If you're trying to turn this into one of your father's sermons, forget it."

"No one's trying to—"

"There's more to life than God and the Bible, you

know." My voice had gotten loud again. I fought to bring it down. "Sometimes people have to take responsibility for their own actions."

She looked at me, then looked down, slowly nodding.

Alright, I'd lost it. Maybe if I'd chosen a less public spot. Maybe if I was more sensitive, understanding. Maybe if— No. I was not on trial here. I wasn't the one who created this mess.

I said nothing more. Just waited.

She kept staring at her cup.

Finally, I spoke. "That's it then?"

She nodded, then quietly repeated, "For now."

Well, she was right about one thing. I'd had enough. I scooted back the chair and rose. "I'll get your coat."

"I think I'll stay here a while."

"I'm sorry, what?"

"You go ahead. I'll find a ride."

"It's freezing cold out there."

"I'll be fine."

"C'mon. I drove you here, it's my responsibility to—"

"No, Joey. It's not." She looked up at me, those blue eyes, gentle but piercing. "I'm not your responsibility."

I stared. Noticed how cold the shop had become.

She looked back at her coffee. "I'll find a ride."

"Mary—"

Her voice was so quiet, I almost missed it. "I managed for eleven months, I can manage now." She said nothing more, just kept staring at her coffee.

"Alright, fine." I turned and started for the door. "Call me if you need me."

If she answered, I didn't hear as I shoved open the door and felt the cold blast of winter hit my face.

FIVE

It wasn't hard breaking into the school that night. The moon was almost full. As long as I stayed out of sight from the street, I'd be fine. If I was lucky, Mrs. Sanford was still having her hot flashes which meant she still taught near the window which she always kept open a crack and usually forgot to lock at night.

I was lucky.

Once inside, it was a quick jog through the halls, lit only by exit signs, and into the gym. High above the polished floor, the skylights filtered in just enough blue-gray light to see my way around. So many memories. And smells . . . old wood, floor polish, the faint whiff of gym clothes from the adjacent locker room.

I crossed to the far end, the last set of folded up bleachers. And there, carved into the third row of seats, visible only to those who knew where to look, were the initials...

J S
+
M M

I ran my fingers over them.

It had been Friday night after one of my games. She'd hung back, waiting for me. Somehow, we were the last ones in the gym. And as a sixteen-year-old, proving my undying love, I'd whipped out my Swiss Army knife and began to carve.

"Joey, what are you doing?"

"Shh, nobody will know."

"But—"

It was probably the only act of vandalism in her entire life. And though she protested and tried to stop me, she didn't try too hard. It became our little secret, and more times than I could remember, our rendezvous point. It stayed here throughout the rest of our high school. And apparently longer.

"Do not be afraid to take Mary home as your wife."

The phrase never faded from my thoughts. If anything, it got louder—during the fiasco at Starbucks, then my drive to our other special place on the river, and later, at the tennis courts where I used to watch her lose match after match, but where she never stopped trying. I even swung by her father's church and parked a few minutes.

"What is conceived in her is from the Holy Spirit."

What did that mean? It made no sense. Then again, as far as I was concerned, that was right up God's alley. Not that I didn't believe in Him. But to try and figure him out? Just ask Charlie Riordan, another Bible thumper. Charlie Riordan, who at this moment was in a California hospital fighting for his life. Charlie Riordan, who despite his God talk, became my best friend in boot camp and served in my unit . . . until Charlie Riordan, without a second's hesitation, threw himself between me and some kid firing a Kalashnikov.

"She will give birth to a son and you are to give him the name

Jesus because he will save his people from their sins."

I shook my head. I stuffed my hands into my pockets and strolled out onto the floor. The place, once full of cheers and life, was now silent and dead. I don't know how long I stood there before I heard the ball roll across the floor. A basketball heading directly for me. I turned, put out my foot to stop it, then peered into the shadows. At first I saw nothing.

"You still got it, kid?"

I smiled. The voice was impossible to forget—the wheezing, smoke-cured voice of Mr. Coghill.

The overhead lights clicked on and an old man in coveralls waddled into view—slightly stooped, fifty pounds overweight, with just a few remaining wisps of flyaway hair. "The war hero still know how to throw up a three pointer?" he asked.

I winced at the phrase, but let it slide. We always let things slide with Mr. Coghill. He'd been the janitor there for as long as anyone can remember. Crotchety, short-tempered, but with the ability to see through any smoke screen—teacher's or student's. What he lacked in grace, and believe me he lacked plenty, he made up with unflinching honesty. Which is probably why the administration kept him around.

Either that or they were afraid to fire him.

"Aren't you dead yet?" I asked.

After a deep, hacking cough, he answered, "Not for lack of trying."

"Those cigarettes just aren't doing the trick?"

"Jack Daniel's a wash, too."

Everyone knew Coghill had a drinking problem, but he never brought it on campus. And he was quick to spot and bust any kid who did . . . then give the kid no rest if he thought he had a problem. Another reason they kept him around.

"So, take a shot," he said.

I glanced down at the basketball, then picked it up and bounced it a couple times, the sound echoing against the bleachers and walls.

"Heard you swung by Leroy's last night," he said.

I shook my head in wonder. "Is there anything you don't know?"

"Small town. Don't be a wus, take a shot."

I looked up to the basket. I was at the top of the key. I took a couple more bounces and fired. *Whoosh*. All net, no rim. First satisfaction I'd had all day. I strolled to the ball, scooped it up and dribbled over to the left of the key.

"She's a good kid," he said. "'Course you know that. And way out of your league."

I set and shot. "Which is why she's having someone else's kid," I said. It hit the rim and bounced off.

He gave no answer.

I retrieved the ball and dribbled it up to the foul line. As casually as possible I asked, "So do you know who the father is?"

Again, no answer.

I shot. Missed. And crossed over to pick it up, again.

"You remember when you boys won District? Right here in this gymnasium." He broke into more coughing. "Remember?"

I didn't bother to reply. Of course I remembered. It was one of the high points of my senior year.

"What was the score again?"

"Eighty-three to eighty-two," I said.

"Yes sir, one fine game. I remember it like it was yesterday. Course you weren't the star that day. Didn't make the winning point."

I started to answer, but he cut me off.

"Jacobson, wasn't it? The new kid. Two seconds left. You were under the basket, could a gone up for an easy layup."

"'Cept their center, Bobby Smoke, was all over me."

"But you was right there. The logical thing to do was try. But no, you passed it to Jacobson, way over there on the base line."

"He was good."

"He was new. Less than a week on the team."

I dribbled back to the foul line. "He proved himself in practice. I figured he could deliver."

"And you were right."

I expected more from the old timer but that was it. I turned to see him standing there, waiting for me to take the bait. Like I had a choice. "So, tell me, Obie-Wan . . . what great lesson am I supposed to learn from that?"

"Nothin' I can think of."

I shot another miss and headed back for the ball.

"Trust's a tricky thing," he said. "'Specially when it comes to the big stuff."

I picked up the ball, looked over to him.

"But if a person's proved themselves in the little things, sometimes you gotta let 'em have the ball in the big things. Even if it don't make sense. If you know 'em, really know 'em, sometimes it's just a matter of trust."

I stared. Message delivered loud and clear.

"Glad you're home, kid." He turned and hobbled toward the exit. "Stay out of trouble."

"That's it. That's all you've got to say?"

"Oh…" He slowed to a stop.

I braced myself.

"Turn out the lights when you're done." He continued toward the doors. "And close your mouth. Makes you look stupider than you are."

SIX

The second morning was worse than the first.

Sleep might have helped, but it wasn't in the cards. I lay on top of the covers, still in my jeans and sweatshirt, staring at the ceiling of my attic bedroom. Thoughts and conversations kept churning, no, make that, roaring, inside my head.

"You know what they say about preacher kids . . . do not be afraid to take Mary as your wife . . . way out of your league . . . she will give birth to a son . . . it's not an it, it's a he . . . I never did like that family . . . everybody loves Mary . . . what is conceived in her is from the Holy Spirit . . ."

It wasn't 'til five, maybe six in the morning that I got around to remembering the Bible verse she had tried to quote. Isaiah seven, something-or-other.

I rolled out of bed, grabbed a Bible off the shelf, the one Mary had given me, and sat down at my little desk in front of the dormer window. The sky was just starting to smear with blue and pink. I found Isaiah, then chapter seven. The beginning wasn't so helpful, all about some king afraid of another king, and this and that, and none of it making much sense.

Until I got to the verse where God talks to a guy named Ahaz:

> "Ask the Lord your God for a sign, whether in the deepest depths or in the highest heights."

'A sign.' Now that was something I could use. Yeah, I know there was the dream, and that was a big deal. The fact I remembered every detail made it even bigger. But still . . .

I stared back out the window, thinking . . . and praying. "Look, God, I don't want to be disrespectful or anything, but I could sure use a hand here. Nothing big. It's not like I need to see a burning bush or anything, but just, you know . . ."

Now don't laugh, but I literally sat there. Just waiting. Listening.

And, big surprise, I got . . . nothing.

I sighed, looked back down at the book and kept reading. Two sentences later it hit me:

> "Therefore the Lord himself will give you a sign: The virgin will conceive and give birth to a son, and will call him Immanuel."

I blinked, stared at the page as the angel's words rushed in:

"What is conceived in her is from the Holy Spirit . . . she will give birth to a son."

Then my conversation with Mary:

"It's not an it. It's a he."

"You've done the tests?"

"I just know."

I looked back at the page.

> "—and will call him Immanuel."

I frowned. Strange name. But no stranger than:

"—and you shall call his name Jesus."

I thought a moment then reached over and fired up the computer. I logged on and, just for fun, Googled the name: Immanuel.

Its meaning? "God with us."

I thought another moment, then entered the name: Jesus.

Its meaning? "God saves."

Not a perfect match, but both talked about God. Maybe it was something. Maybe not. But I was getting closer. To what, I wasn't sure. I closed my eyes, trying to remember what else Mary had said:

"You know in the Bible, all those prophecies talking about a great leader that's going to come?"

I'd heard about this leader my whole life. Some dude who's supposed to save the world, solve all our problems. Not that I paid much attention. You hear stuff like that enough times and pretty soon you don't hear it at all.

I decided to Google what this great leader was supposed to do and . . . well, there went the rest of my morning.

There were hundreds of links on this guy. And plenty of nut jobs claiming to be him. There were also plenty of references about him in the Bible. And it seemed everyone and everybody had an opinion. Most figured he'd be a great political leader, come to straighten out the mess we're in. Others said he'd be a prophet, like in the Bible, only bigger. A few on the fringe even said he was supposed to suffer and die—which was pretty ridiculous since how do you save a world by suffering and dying?

But no matter how much I searched, my mind kept going back to that verse Mary had given me.

"Therefore the Lord himself will give you a sign: The virgin will conceive and give birth to a son, and will call him Immanuel."

And to what the angel had said: *"What is conceived in her is from the Holy Spirit. She will give birth to a son and you are to give him the name Jesus because he will save his people from their sins."*

Suddenly, out of the blue, Coghill's words swept in: *"If you know 'em, really know 'em, sometimes it's just a matter of trust."*

Know them. That was the key. *Really know them.* I didn't have the facts, and if I did, I was clueless how to put them together. But I knew Mary. I knew who she was. There was little the two of us hadn't shared.

"Sometimes it's just a matter of trust."

I glanced at the time. 9:25. She'd be up now. I pulled out my cell and hit speed dial, hoping she'd take my call. There were still a thousand questions to answer, but maybe now, like she said, maybe now I might at least be able to listen.

My call went to her message. "Hi, it's Mary. I'm out, you're on." *Beep.*

I hung up and looked out the window. That's when I noticed Dad's pickup in the driveway. What was he doing home? Shouldn't he be at work? Shouldn't he— Wait a minute. It was Sunday. Sunday morning. And that meant church. She'd be at church in–the clock clicked to 9:26–four minutes!

I leaped from my chair, grabbed my coat and scarf, and stumbled down the stairs. Incidentals like a shower or changing clothes never crossed my mind. We had to talk.

And I . . . I had to listen.

SEVEN

I shot through town pretty fast, one hand on the wheel, the other wiping away fog that kept coming back on the inside of the windshield. (The pickup's defroster worked as good as its heater). Up ahead, our one stoplight blinked red. My side windows were coated in ice so I rolled them down to see as I blew through the intersection. If old man McDermott was anything, he was punctual.

I slid into a parking spot at 9:38.

I half-ran, half-slipped along the sidewalk. I took the steps two at a time and could hear them singing one of those chorus songs that keep repeating. Definitely not McDermott's favorite. He liked the old-fashioned hymns. "Something with depth and meaning." But that's not what his little flock wanted. And forcing them to do something wasn't his style. When possible, he liked to nudge folks, but never force them. Despite his rigid, button-down ways, he was gentle and sensitive. You could see it in his eyes.

And in his oldest daughter.

I yanked open the door. It was a small church. More

like a chapel. Exposed beams in the ceiling, about a dozen rows of wooden pews, and worn green carpet running down the aisle. Up front, sitting on a stool, with his guitar and dreadlocks, sat worship leader, Joel Lambert. Behind him was an altar of polished ash. To his left a matching pulpit. And to his right hung the mandatory screen displaying the mandatory PowerPoint of lyrics.

My entrance startled Mr. Swenson. The old guy sat at the back so he could usher. Actually, that's not true. Yes, he was the usher—he'd been doing that for as long as Mary could remember—but the truth is, he sat back there so he could doze off without anyone noticing. Anyone but the pastor who never called him on it. Like I said, McDermott was a thoughtful man.

Swenson struggled to his feet but I motioned him to stay put. I knew where I was going. He did, too. I looked to the front. There was no way of sneaking past the congregation unnoticed. By now, everyone was locked in place, including the McDermotts . . . all four of them in the first row.

I sucked it up and started down the aisle.

Heads turned, looks were traded. I pretended not to see, keeping my eyes up front until I reached McDermott's pew. That's when I turned around and saw every eye of the congregation on me. I should have charged admission.

Mrs. McDermott, a handsome, graying version of her daughter, sat on the end. When she saw me, her face lit up with that big welcoming grin of hers—before stealing a nervous glance down the row to Mary who must have noticed but kept right on singing. Next to Mrs. McDermott stood her husband. As I passed, we traded nods . . . before he arched an eyebrow at my wrinkled clothes and uncombed hair. He probably wasn't crazy about the smell, either. After him came twelve-year old Rachel, all knees and elbows, who gave a quiet squeal of delight as she threw her arms around me.

That left Mary.

I freed myself from Rachel and looked to her. She gave a polite smile and stepped to the side, making room for me between her and Rachel. That was it. No fanfare. No drama. I don't know what I was expecting, but she continued singing like she wasn't the least bit surprised. Maybe she wasn't.

I found my place in the song and joined in—my heart giving a tiny leap as she silently slipped her arms through mine.

EIGHT

"How did you know it was an angel?"

"I think it was the name tag," she said.

"You're kidding me."

Mary gave me a look. I guess she was.

She stared back out the pickup's windshield. It was after church and we were at our spot on the river, next to the leaning cottonwood, its lowest branch skimming the icy water. This was where we'd parked on cold winter nights, sharing our dreams and fears. Where we picnicked on summer afternoons, planning our future, debating how many children we'd have—she wanted three, four, five; I figured two would be enough–and, of course, where we decided their sexes.

This was where she'd cried when I told her my need to serve our country. And this was where we both wept the night she said yes and accepted my ring.

Now, under the afternoon's slate-gray sky, she explained what little she knew . . .

"I was sitting over there, on that big rock above the water, when suddenly he's beside me. One minute I'm all alone, the next he's standing above me—tall, NBA tall, dressed in white—white jeans, white tee-shirt, everything white, so white he's almost glowing."

"Were you scared?" I asked.

She cut me a look.

Another stupid question.

She continued. "And then he spoke. Real gentle, but powerful. Soft, but roaring like a waterfall." She got quiet, obviously remembering. Finally, she went on. "'Greetings,' he said, 'you who are highly favored. The Lord is with you.'" She frowned. "It made no sense but I was too scared to speak."

"Because you thought it was an angel."

"Because I knew it was an angel."

I nodded.

She cocked her head to the side, still remembering, but with a growing sense of wonder. "He said, 'Do not be afraid, Mary. You have found favor with God. You will conceive and give birth to a son, and you are to call him Jesus.'"

"Jesus?" I asked. "You sure he said to name him, Jesus?"

She nodded. "Why?

"Because that's the same thing I heard in my dream. 'You are to give him the name Jesus.'"

She looked at me, eyes widening. I nodded.

She turned back to the windshield, quietly continuing, "'He will be great and will be called the Son of the Most High.'"

"'Of the Most High,'" I softly repeated.

If she heard, she didn't answer. She was too lost in the memory. Her voice became a whisper, "'But how?' I asked him. 'I'm still a virgin. How can I possibly have a son?' And he said, 'The Holy Spirit will come on you, and the power of the Most High will overshadow you. So, the holy one to be born will be called the Son of God.'"

I felt the hair on my arms rise.

We sat in the silence, trying to grasp it all. She shivered and scooted closer. I fired up the car, grateful the heater decided to cooperate. I wrapped an arm around her, and she continued:

"But he wasn't done."

I waited, knowing she'd go on when she was ready.

"'Elizabeth,' he said. 'Your relative, Elizabeth, who has been unable to conceive is going to have a child in her old age. Even now, she's in her sixth month." Mary paused, then repeated the next words with emphasis. "'For no word from God will ever fail.'"

I finally spoke. "Elizabeth, your aunt? The one you visited?"

She nodded.

"And?"

"Their baby boy just celebrated his five-month birthday."

I swore softly. Probably not the right response when talking about God and angels and miracles, but I'd pretty much run out of words.

"So what did you do?" I asked. "What did you say?"

Her voice thickened with emotion—part fear, part awe, but also that quiet determination of hers. "I said, 'I am the Lord's servant. May your word to me be fulfilled.'"

I don't know how long we sat there, or what we said, if anything. I mean what could you say? All I remember was thinking, if this is true, and it seemed to be, then Mary had done her part. She had agreed and she had obeyed.

Now it was time for me to step up and do mine.

NINE

I didn't expect my dad to believe, and he didn't.

Miracle dreams and guest appearances by angels were just a little too much to swallow. Nobody doubted God could part the Red Sea or perform all that other stuff in the Bible . . . He just never did it today, not on our watch.

That didn't mean Dad didn't support us. He liked Mary. And, if in her naive innocence, she'd been seduced by some guy and was now doing her best to protect him, well, that was her business. And mine. If it's what I wanted, Dad would be there to watch my back . . . even if it meant punching out some punk at the mill.

The thought still made me smile.

And Mom? She was a tougher sell. Still, she did her best to be civil—even when she felt her boy was falling for a line of . . . well, she was too polite to use the real phrase, but we all knew what she meant when she said, "Bovine feces."

The wedding would be small, not because of embarrassment, but because that was Mary's style. A quiet celebration with just her family and closest friends. Yes, there would be flowers and music and whatever else our two mothers needed, but for Mary all she wanted was to be with those she loved in the church she loved. Oh, and to be married in her mother's wedding dress. As a little girl, more than once she'd been busted for sneaking into the back of her mom's closet and trying it on. Sure, they'd have to make a few alterations, particularly in the baby bump area, but she'd asked for so little—to be married in the dress of the woman she loved, by the father she loved, in the church she loved.

It was that last point that started all the problems . . .

Not with her dad. To be honest, McDermott probably felt like he was eating crow every time he stepped out the front door. But he never stopped believing in us — even without the help of angels. No, it wasn't the good Pastor, it was his church—less than two weeks before the wedding.

According to McDermott, the leaders or deacons or whatever they're called, had summoned him to an emergency meeting. When he got there, they were already sitting around, sober-faced, at a long table down in the church's kitchen. Six men. No women. Brent Wilson, the head guy, broke the news. He was perfectly dressed like he always was—wool sweater, color coordinated tie, freshly pressed Dockers . . . and a face so scrubbed it practically glowed. "I'm sorry, Pastor," he said. "But as much as we love you and your family, as much as we support your leadership, we cannot allow the wedding of your daughter to be performed on the premises."

McDermott, a poker player though he'd never touched a card, simply looked at him. "Because?" he asked.

Wilson answered, "Because of the testimony to the community, to the members of the church."

Martin Henderson, taller, thinner, but just as scrubbed, added, "It's imperative we don't give the impression that we are somehow endorsing pre-marital sex."

McDermott answered, "No one here's endorsing—"

"Exactly," Wilson said. "To hold a ceremony on the premises as if there was nothing in the world wrong with that type of behavior sends a message that neither you, nor the congregation would want to endorse."

"But kids are having babies out of wedlock every day," McDermott said.

"My point exactly."

"That doesn't mean we're endorsing it. No one's endorsing it. *Mary* isn't endorsing it."

Wilson looked down at the table. Cleared his throat. "Mary is a role model for the young people in this church. Teaching Sunday school since she was in middle school, working with the youth—"

Henderson eagerly interrupted. "A role model for the entire community."

Others around the table agreed.

Wilson continued, "All the more reason we have to be careful how we handle this . . . situation."

McDermott sat there, waiting. He figured there was more, and he wasn't wrong.

Wilson continued. "That's why we feel there is a solution. I mean we all know how much your daughter loves this church, how devoted she is to-"

"A solution?" McDermott said.

"Yes."

"Which is?"

"If Mary would come before the congregation. If she would stand before the congregation and publically confess her sin, if she would make it clear that—"

"No."

"Make it clear that her behavior was—"

"No."

Wilson stopped, didn't have to wait long for clarification.

"My daughter will not be publicly humiliated."

Looks were traded around the table.

Henderson pressed in. "Pastor, what we are offering is a reasonable solution that everyone—"

"My daughter will not be put on display."

Wilson chose his words carefully. "Every day your daughter comes to this church she is on display."

McDermott took a deep breath. He told me later that he'd almost lost it. But I guess you learn a few things about patience being a pastor all those years. "Brent," he kept his voice calm and even. "You and I, we started this church . . . 24 years ago from a small Bible study in my home. We've poured our lives into it. My family has poured their lives—"

"No one here is doubting your sacrifice."

McDermott looked around the table. "I've married some of you here. And your kids. Josh, we just buried your mother." Eyes faltered, examined the top of the table. "Mary grew up in this church. You're our family."

Silence, except for Wilson's quiet cough.

"No." McDermott shook his head. "You will not make an example of my daughter. You will not shame her in front of the congregation to satisfy—"

"Your daughter has already done that," Henderson said. "She's already shamed herself."

Talk about a low blow. McDermott could have easily exploded, thrown a chair or two, turned over a table. But he didn't. Somehow, he kept it together. He never told us the rest of the story. Or how the meeting ended. But they should be grateful it was him sitting across that table and not my old man. Or me.

Later that evening, when he broke the news, when we all sat in his living room, Mary never said a word.

She nodded, she briefly touched her eyes, and that was that. I didn't learn 'til later that ever since middle school she'd been secretly rehearsing walking down the aisle of the church.

The news broke Mary's heart. But not her faith.

And mine? I wasn't sure what it did. It certainly didn't make me a fan of church goers. And God? All I could do was ask, "*Why? Why, if she was so special, if He loved her so much, why did He make things so hard?*"

He never answered. At least then. And it only got worse.

Another week passed. We'd agreed to have the ceremony in the old grange hall. Same guests, same decorations, same dress . . . until the registered letter from McDermott's denominational headquarters arrived. Brent Wilson and his band of self-righteous twits were not content to bar the wedding from the church. They used the same arguments to bar McDermott from performing the wedding:

"An embarrassment to the denomination," the letter said. "An endorsement of sin." But something that could, "easily be remedied if Mary would simply confess her sin, if not publically, then in an open letter to the congregation."

That's when McDermott hit the ceiling. He may have a longer fuse than me or Dad, but the explosion was just as intense.

He called for another family meeting—same living room, same chairs, same sofa, but with the addition of a lit powder keg. The man's voice wasn't any louder, but the bulging veins in his neck and the crimson red of his cheeks said things had definitely escalated.

Mrs. McDermott saw the clues, tried in vain to settle him down. "I'm sure Reverend Katzenberger, just down the street, would step in," she said. "He's been a friend since before Mary was born."

“No.” His voice was ominously quiet.

“Or Dr. Cooke, we always enjoy having him—”

“No.”

“Sweetheart.” There was no missing her concerned tone. “We can’t—”

“I am marrying my daughter.”

“But—”

“It’s what we’ve always planned, it’s what we will do.”

I felt Mary’s body tense beside me. “Dad,” she said, “it’s not important enough to go against the Council. You know what they’ll—”

“No.”

“I’m just saying it’s—”

“I will marry my daughter.” He still didn’t shout, but somehow his voice was louder than if he had. And that’s when I began understanding where Mary got her will.

“Mrs. McDermott tried one final time. “If they defrock you, if they take away your license, what—”

“Enough!” This time he did shout. More of a roar. “The wedding is in 48 hours and nothing will stop me from marrying my daughter!”

The room grew silent.

But there *was* something that would stop him. Something even stronger than his love, his iron will . . . and even his faith.

TEN

Mary's love. That was the only thing that could stop her father.

The next day, eighteen hours before the wedding, I was kneeling in gray, gritty slush alongside Highway 12, fixing a flat on my pickup. I'd dropped a lug nut from my numb fingers and was digging through the mush to find it. Mary stood behind me in the falling snow, hands stuffed in her jacket, plumes of breath around her head. She'd just undergone a mild contraction and wanted to be outside to stand. She said it was nothing to worry about, some women get them two to three months ahead of time. Apparently, she was one of the lucky ones. Still, it was a first for me and a bit alarming.

As I dug through the slush, she asked, "Need a hand?"

"Nah, I'm good," I said. "You sure you're okay?"

"I'm good," she repeated.

But, of course, neither of us was good. I felt like a traitor. And Mary? I can't imagine what she felt. But the decision had been made and we were following through. Two hours earlier, at St. Arbucks, she had sprung it on me.

"It's just a ceremony," she'd said.

"It's something you've waited for your entire life."

"No."

"Yes."

"Joey . . . I waited my entire life for you. Not the ceremony. The ceremony is just a . . . formality."

She was a terrible liar. Never had the practice. Her eyes shifted to the counter, then stared out the window, anywhere but to mine. She was desperate to save her father's reputation, not to mention his job, and she'd do anything necessary for him to keep it. "If we leave right now we could make it over to the courthouse before they close."

"Mar—"

"We've already got the license. But we have to leave now. They close at 5:00 and it's a two-hour drive.

I shook my head.

"Why not?" she said.

"Our parents, our friends—"

"We'll still have the reception. It'll be exactly the same, except—"

"Except you're sacrificing everything you ever dreamed about in a wedding."

"If we don't do it, Dad will sacrifice everything he's ever dreamed and worked for."

I watched as she looked back out the window, back to the counter, down at her coffee. It was dueling love . . . a father's love verses his daughter's.

"Joey." She turned back to me. "I've dreamed about becoming your wife before you even knew I existed."

"Oh, I knew."

"And marrying you will be the happiest day of my life. But if we don't do something for Daddy, it'll also be my saddest."

Daddy. In all our time together, I'd never heard her use that term. *Daddy*. Coming from her at that time, in that place, it made her sound so fragile, desperate . . . child-like. I could have fought her. After all, it was my wedding, too. But who was I kidding? This was Mary. To go against her on this would be going against her very core—the very thing that made her who she was—that grabbed my heart and had never let it go.

Still, maybe I should have said no. I'd thought about it a dozen times as we headed off into the growing snow flurries. I thought about it as Mary texted her mom then turned off the phone so she wouldn't get back the protesting response. Yes, I thought about it. But, like her father, like his daughter, love seemed to be winning out.

It wasn't until I tossed the jack behind the seat and helped Mary up into the cab that I realized it still wasn't done with us. I glanced at my watch. 4:42. I slid behind the wheel to coax the pickup into starting and Mary said what we were both thinking.

"We're not going to make it now, are we?"

I looked out the windshield. The snow was falling faster. Wet and heavy. I sighed and shook my head. "Not in this weather."

We sat a moment in silence.

"Maybe it's a sign," I said. "Maybe God's telling us to head home and go ahead with the— What are you doing?"

She'd pulled out her cell phone and checked something.

"Mary?"

She read the screen. "The Courthouse opens at 10:00 AM."

"Mar-"

"No, listen. The clerk could marry us tomorrow."

"But the reception. In this snow we'll never get back in time for—"

"It's just a reception. Besides, not that many people are coming."

"Come on, it's important."

"We can make it up to them. Throw a big pot luck next week. Or the week after." She was determined, though her voice was thickening with emotion. "That way we'd have more time to spend with them, one on one and . . . and, I think that's what we should do."

She looked out the passenger window. If she hadn't given her cheek a quick brush, I'd have never known she was crying.

"Mary . . ."

Still looking away, she nodded. "It's the right thing to do."

I waited, watched. She gave another nod, repeated more softly. "It's the right thing."

It was settled. I knew her mind was made up. I knew something else, too. Her love had just raised the stakes . . . and, once again, it had won.

I dropped the truck into gear, and pulled back onto the highway.

ELEVEN

Just to be safe, Mary had called the courthouse to make an appointment for the following morning at 10:00 sharp. We came rolling in at about 11:05. Besides a rough night's sleep at the nearby Motel 6 (two rooms, my idea, not hers), there was a trip to Target to pick up some makeup and other odds and ends (her idea, not mine). Girls, go figure.

The snow had been coming down steadily all night and the temperature had dropped to near zero. We were grateful to step into the warmth of the old, historical building that smelled of dusty books and floor wax. Not so grateful when we met the county clerk, a Napoleon wannabe, with thick eyeglasses, stationed behind the counter.

"We're late," I said.

Carefully eyeballing Mary, he answered with what he must have thought was humor. "By about nine months."

I let it go. "Can you still squeeze us in?" I asked.

He motioned to the empty lobby—empty benches, empty clerk windows, not a soul in sight.

"Great," I said. "So where do we go, what do we do?"

"You have a witness?"

"A . . . witness?" I looked to Mary who frowned. This was news to both of us.

He pushed up his glasses. "Not official without a witness."

Behind him two workers were hunched over their computers. "What about one of those—"

"County employees." He busied himself with papers. "Can't go stopping every time some kids think they want to legalize their sex."

Mary sensed my anger and touched my arm as a caution. I pulled it together. She was right. This was the little man's little fiefdom and there was no use trying to wrench it from him. But even then, I was back to thinking, *why?* It was the same question I'd struggled with ever since Charlie Riordan got hit, since I first heard the news about Mary. *Why, if God had so much love, why was He so hard on those who loved Him the most?*

I'd barely finished the thought before something behind us caught the little man's eye. "Ah, you're in luck."

I turned, following his gaze past the lobby to the double doors where an old, familiar couple and their daughter entered.

"Momma?" Mary gasped. "Dad?"

"There they are!" Rebecca cried as she spotted us. She raced across the floor, leaving plenty of watery tracks and a scowl on the clerk's face.

"What . . . what are you guys doing here?" Mary asked as Rebecca hugged her.

Her sister giggled mischievously and turned to hug

me.

McDermott's voice boomed from the doors as he stomped the snow off his feet. "Terrible weather out there."

"We're not too late, are we?" Mrs. McDermott asked.

"No, Momma." Mary grinned. She gave her cheek another brush. "You're right on time."

And that's when it hit me — my question about God's love. Maybe, just maybe the greatest love comes wrapped in the greatest difficulties. The idea was supported by something else as well. It looked like the clerk would have to wait just a little bit longer before starting the ceremony. Because there, folded over Mrs. McDermott's arm, was her wedding dress.

TWELVE

Mary's folks sprang for three days at the local Holiday Inn in Chehalis. Their wedding gift to us, as if they hadn't given enough already.

"Cool," Rebecca called from across the hotel's lobby. She'd already scored a free oatmeal cookie from the front desk, poked around the lobby with its fake-log fireplace, and checked out the Photo-shopped pictures of blurry streams and waterfalls. Now she spotted the swimming pool across the hall from the elevators. "Can we stay, too?"

"No way," McDermott said as he finished signing at the desk.

She half-skipped, half twirled back to us, focusing on her mom. "Please . . ."

Mrs. McDermott chuckled. "That's up to Mary and Joe."

She turned to us. "We won't disturb you. *Please . . .*"

Mary shook her head. "I love you squirt, but Dad's

right, no way."

"What about just me? I could hang out way at the other end of the hall or even the other floor. You wouldn't even know I'm here."

We traded amused looks.

"*Pleeease . . .*"

Then, like some TV sitcom, we answered in perfect unison, "No way!"

I won't go into detail about our wedding night—though I can tell you, out of respect for what was growing inside her, we had agreed not to, as the Bible says, *know one another*. Even at that, as we got ready for bed, we were painfully self-conscious, giggling like school kids. I can also tell you my feelings as I watched her finally slip into sleep, the gentle rise and fall of her shoulders under the amber parking lot lights diffused through window sheers. Actually, I just had one feeling. Awe. Awe over the strength of this woman/child whose back was nestled into me. Awe, that she was protecting and pouring her life into the making of another. Awe, that with my arms wrapped around her, my fingertips were just inches from an entirely different life that was forming at millions of cells per second. And awe at how that life had already, and would no doubt, continue to change our lives.

If I slept, I can't tell you when. The time was too precious to miss a second. But the sheers slowly turned from amber to dull white. And that's when my phone rang. I tried to catch it before it woke her, but managed only to fumble it from the nightstand to the carpet. I slipped out of bed and dropped to my knees to answer in a whisper.

"Hello?"

"Joseph?" A woman's voice. Ragged and breathy.

"Yes."

"Joseph Shepherd?"

"Who's this?"

"Dorothy Riordan."

My mind raced, trying to place the name.

"Charlie's mom," she said. "Charlie Riordan?"

Charlie Riordan, my buddy. The one who, despite my mistake, had risked his life to save mine. "Mrs. Riordan. How are you? How is he?"

"He's, uh, he's asking for you."

"For me?"

Mary stirred. "Joey," she mumbled, "what's wrong?"

"Nothing, babe, go back to sleep."

I bent lower to the floor, spoke softer. "He's asking for me?

"He's taken a turn for the worse, and, uh. . ." The phone rustled.

"Mrs. Riordan?"

"Joey?" Mary struggled to turn, rose up on one elbow. "What are you doing? Who are you talking to?"

Mrs. Riordan came back on. "I'm not sure what time it is where you are, and I know it's a terrible inconveniencc—"

"No, no," I said, "What can I do?"

"He's asking for you."

"Can you put him on?"

"He had a pretty rough night. He's sleeping now. But he wanted to know, he's asking, I know it's a terrible inconvenience…"

"Please, what can I do?"

Mary moved across the bed until she was looking down at me.

"He's asking, he wants. . ."

And then it hit me. "He wants me to visit him?"

"That's . . . that's what he's asking."

My mind raced. I saw Mary trying to read my expression.

"When?" I said.

"I know it's an inconvenience, but—"

No, no," I rubbed my forehead, "It's no problem. Where is he? What hospital?"

"No, he's home," Mrs. Riordan said. "He wanted to be here when he, uh . . . he wanted to come home."

"So it's serious."

"We'll pay for the flight. Only . . ."

I finished her thought. ". . . the sooner the better."

"They said, they said he just has a few days."

I rose to my knees, opened the nightstand drawer searching for a pad and pencil. "Okay, and the address, can you give me your address?"

Mary turned and grabbed them off her nightstand.

"I know it's a terrible inconvenience, and I wouldn't ask—"

"No, no, I understand."

Mary handed me the paper and pencil. I nodded a thanks.

"And your address?" I said.

We're an hour outside of Fresno. We can fly you into Fresno and pick you up—"

"No, that's okay," I said. "I can rent a car. And your address?"

She gave it to me and again apologized for the inconvenience. I assured her it was no problem, that I'd be down there ASAP. I owed him that. I owed him more than that.

We said goodbye and I hung up. Only when I looked up to see Mary staring quizzically down at me, did I realize how 'inconvenient' it really was. Because now, I wasn't just making decisions for one person, it was two.

Make that three.

THIRTEEN

Joey, can you slow down a little?"

"I did," I said.

"Which is why we're back up to what, 70, again?

"If we're going to make it down to Portland before the storm hits, we've got to move."

Mary said nothing which was like saying everything which meant it was my turn again. "We're being looked out for, remember?" I reached down to her hand. "God's not going to let anything happen to us. If He said all those things about the baby then—" I stopped as the high beams appeared in my mirror along with the flashing blue and red lights.

Somehow, I managed not to cuss.

Mary searched my face then turned to see a Washington State Patrol car signaling for us to pull over. I braked and moved through the slower lanes. His car remained glued to my tail, until we came to a stop in the emergency lane.

"Great," I said, throwing the truck into Park. "Just great."

Mary had good reason to say plenty. She also had the good sense not to. Another plus in her column.

"Can you hand me the registration?" I said. "There should be an insurance card in there, too."

She opened the glove compartment and handed them to me as I waited. And waited. I drummed my fingers on the steering wheel. "You'd think . . ." I stopped, my mind rehashing why we kept having all these little setbacks. Yesterday I thought I had a handle on it. But that was yesterday.

"Think what?" she asked.

"You'd think if we're so special, if your child was-"

"Our child."

"If our child was so special, you'd think the Almighty would cut us a little slack."

She looked silently out the windshield.

"What?" I said.

"Maybe it's *because* he's so special. Maybe that's why we have to do everything by the book. No short cuts. Maybe. . ." She stopped and shook her head, making it clear she didn't know.

I took a breath and blew it out. It was barely ten in the morning and it had already been a long day—starting off with our first, official, newlywed argument. . .

"No," I had called from the bathroom. "Absolutely not."

Mary, who had already dressed, was struggling to put on her shoes. "But I'm your wife."

"All the more reason not to drag you down to California."

"Chehalis is already half way to Sea-Tac airport." She struggled to stand. "You're not going to drive me all the way back home, then have to turn around and come all the way back. In this weather it will take you forever."

"No. You can stay here. Your dad can pick you up."

"He's done enough already."

"He'd understand. He'd—"

"I'm not his responsibility, Joey."

The edge to her voice brought me up short.

She continued, "You and me, we're the ones who signed up for this program. Not my dad. Not anyone else. You. Me."

"I get that, but—"

"I said yes to God. You said yes to God. That's how it has to be." Realizing things were getting heated, she brought it back down. "We're family now. The three of us, we're . . . family."

"No." I grabbed my shirt off the bathroom door hook and slipped it on. "It's too dangerous."

"Dangerous?"

"Pregnant women aren't supposed to fly."

"Since when?"

"Since, since I don't know."

She crossed to the dresser, out of sight.

"Isn't there a rule or something?" I said. "Some cutoff date? I mean what do the doctors say?"

No answer.

"Mary?"

"Thirty-two weeks."

I stepped from the bathroom. She held up her phone, indicating she'd just checked the internet.

"And you're at thirty," I said.

"Going on thirty-one."

"See? That's way too close."

"Says who?"

I chose not to answer.

"Joey, it's within the limit."

"Why take the risk?"

"There is no risk, not if we're within the limit. Not if

we. . ." She hesitated.

"Not if we what?"

"Not if we trust God."

I shot her a look. She cocked her head, waiting for a comeback.

I didn't disappoint. "You can't go around always playing the God card."

"And why is that?"

"Because . . . because . . ." I searched for a reason.

"Seems He had no problem playing it on us," she said.

I closed my eyes, shook my head. I could have kept arguing, used all the human logic in the world. The only problem was we'd entered a world where human logic didn't always seem to apply.

Twenty minutes later I was out in the parking lot scraping snow off the windshield, pouring hot water on the wipers to unfreeze them, and coaxing both truck and heater into working.

Ten minutes after that, with the rhythmic *woosh-woosh* of wipers and the hum of tires, we were heading north on the I-5 to Sea-Tac International Airport. Mary sat beside me, working her cell phone and my credit card until she'd finally scored some tickets. They weren't the cheapest and our seats would be separate, but it looked like we were a go.

"Actually," she said, "this could be a good thing."

"How so?"

"Think of it as an extended honeymoon."

"What, three days at the Chehalis Holiday Inn isn't enough for you?"

She wrapped an arm around mine. "And free continental breakfasts, don't forget that."

I nodded. "Seriously, what more could a girl want?"

She laid her head on my shoulder. "Guess I'm just high maintenance."

I felt a warmth in my chest spreading through my throat. Here was this lady, beautiful, my best friend, someone who always looked for the good in everything. She deserved so much better than this, than me. But here we were, heading down a road neither of us could imagine . . . one, with more than its fair share of speed bumps.

"Closed," she said less than two minutes later.

I looked to her as she re-checked her phone. "What?"

"That's what it says. The airport is closed. All flights cancelled."

"You mean, delayed."

She checked again and shook her head. "Cancelled."

"Because of a little snow?"

"They're calling it the storm of the century. A big one coming down from Canada."

"Headed this way?"

She nodded.

I scowled as she continued working the phone. Up ahead was Exit 95, the one to Littlerock and Maytown. I paused, then suddenly swerved to the right.

"Joey!"

Drivers expressed their appreciation with blowing horns and the universal road-rage salute.

"What are you doing?

I barely made the exit and started up the ramp. "Portland. Is the Portland airport still open?"

She checked her phone as I pulled to the stop sign and turned left.

"Yes."

"Perfect. If the storm's coming from the north, there's a chance we can hit Portland before it does." I took another left onto the entrance ramp, heading south.

Mary began checking flights.

I picked up speed. "Doesn't have to be Fresno," I said. "Could be Oakland, San Jose, Sacramento."

"On it."

If we hurried I hoped we'd catch something.

Unfortunately, it was the *hurrying* that had thirty minutes later caught the State Patrol's attention. An attention that, once he'd signaled us over to the side of the freeway, seemed anything but in a hurry.

I waited another minute. Maybe two. Having had enough, I reached for the door. But, Mary, once again reading my mind, touched my arm. "Babe."

She was right, of course. Getting out would only cause problems, slow the officer even more. There would be no hurrying him. A fact he seemed to relish. Even more so when he finally approached the car and I rolled down the window.

After a friendly greeting and brief chat about the weather . . .

"Ain't seen nothin' like it. Not in years."

And after we explained we were in a hurry to catch a flight . . .

"Understood. Course, it ain't worth risking a life over now, is it?"

And after taking our license, insurance card and registration . . .

"I'll be back in a jiffy."

And after checking us out on his radio . . .

And after he returned, subjecting us to another brief lecture about automobile safety . . .

"Especially with her being in the family way. And, oh, I'm gonna have to fine you extra for that right broken tail light."

After all that, we were finally on our way.

I'd barely pulled back onto the freeway before Mary looked up from her phone. "Got it," she said. "San Jose International Airport."

"Perfect."

"Not cheap."

I nodded, making sure to signal and obey any other law I could think of while keeping an eye on the State Patrol through my mirror. "We'll take what we can get."

FOURTEEN

"You're kidding me."

"No sir."

"You sell us a flight that you know you're going to cancel—"

"We had no idea the storm would—"

"You had every idea. Everybody in the world knew it was coming."

"Babe." It was another signal from Mary to cool down.

The attendant behind the counter, a Pillsbury Dough Boy with attitude, was trying to go toe to toe with me. On the field I would have made short work of him, but here he held all the cards and he knew it.

Without blinking, he added, "We can put you on standby for the next available flight."

"Standby!"

"Unless you're willing to upgrade to first class." He held his ground. "They're going fast but we still have a few seats—"

"We booked coach."

"Correct, but those seats are already taken."

"You cancel our flight and tell me the only way to get on the next one is to—"

"The weather cancelled your flight, sir. And if you look at the terms of agreement—"

"Weather that you were fully aware of."

Mary's hand was on my arm. But I knew men like this. The only way to win was through intimidation. "Let me speak to your supervisor."

"I am the supervisor."

My heart pounded.

Mary, thinking her sugar and spice approach would work, stepped in. "What time is the next flight?"

A flurry of keystrokes and the attendant answered. "That would be 10:35 tonight." He looked back to me and pushed up his glasses, an obvious challenge.

"We're done here." I grabbed the tickets off the counter.

"Joe . . ."

"I'm not hanging around, making you sit here for the next ten hours just to—"

"He's your friend. He's dying."

"And you're my wife. You're having a baby. We're done." I took her arm, turning from the counter. "I'm taking you home."

"And I have no say?"

I looked to her.

Her jaw was set, the way it gets when she digs in.

"Of course," I said, "but—"

"Then I say we stay."

"Mary."

"Excuse me." It was a tall, gray-haired guy in sports coat and turtle neck. He was next in line behind us. A line much longer than when we started. "If you don't mind, some of us are in a hurry."

"Give us a second," I said.

"Joey, your friend is dying. A man who loves you, needs you."

I turned back to her. "You're not being rational. You're pregnant, you need your rest, you—"

"Rational?" She motioned to her belly. "Since when has any of this been rational? Joey, you love this man."

"And you're my wife. I have a responsibility. I have a—"

She shook her head. "No."

"What?"

"You have a responsibility to love. If you do that, God will take care of the rest."

I tried not to scoff. "Common sense dictates that we—"

"Since when does common sense have anything to do with love?"

I frowned. So we were back to that, were we?

"I love you, Joey."

"And I love you," I stammered.

"Which is why we should go."

She was wrong in so many ways. Wrong, and yet. . .

"Excuse me." It was the turtleneck again. "I hate to break up this soap opera, but—"

I turned on him. "Chill, alright."

"Joey—"

I closed my eyes, turned back to the agent. "How much?"

He told me. I tried not to gasp.

Mary softened the blow. "And you can get us seats together?"

"Yes, ma'am."

"And there'll be snacks?"

"And a gourmet meal."

"With table cloths?"

"Correct."

She turned to me, gave a single nod of satisfaction. Apparently, the deal was sealed. I shook my head, grumbling while pulling out my credit card. Then, as the agent finished draining our blood, a thought came to my mind. "You can get us into the VIP lounge, right?"

"Are you a member?"

"No."

"Then I'm afraid not."

Unbelievable. If the guy wanted to go for a second round I was ready. "Excuse me?" I raised my voice loud enough to be heard a couple counters over. "My wife is having a baby and you don't have the decency to let her stay in your lounge?"

"I'm sorry, sir, but your wife having a baby was neither mine nor the airline's fault. So if—"

I grabbed his hand, squeezing it hard. Breaking it was out of the question, but I could sure put the fear of God into him. I lowered my voice, "Listen, you miserable excuse for a—"

"Ahh!" Mary let out a stifled scream. I turned to see her leaning over the counter.

"What's wrong?" I asked. "Are you alright?"

She nodded, trying to breathe, unable to speak through the pain.

"Ma'am?" the agent asked as I let go of his hand. "Ma'am?"

It was another contraction. This one seeming much harder than the others.

"Ma'am? Are you okay?"

She was finally able to answer, "Yes, I'm fine."

"Are you, that is to say, are you going into—"

She shook her head. "I'll be fine."

"Alright, that's enough," the turtleneck behind us said.

I turned to him, ready to battle two fronts if

necessary. But before I spoke, he reached past me with a credit card of his own. Platinum, of course. "Buy them a membership."

"Sir?" the agent said.

"Look at her, you idiot. Buy them a membership."

"Well . . . if you're certain." The agent took his card.

I turned to the turtleneck, puzzled, not sure how to respond.

"The word you're looking for is, 'thanks.'"

I nodded. "Thanks . . ."

"Anything to get things moving."

By the time they'd finished the transaction, Mary's contraction was over. We started toward the lounge, VIP cards in hand. The agent had the good sense not to wish us a 'good day.'

"Are you okay?" I asked her. "That one seemed pretty strong."

"I'm fine."

"Timing was convenient. Another one of your God things?"

"Could be."

I looked at her. She gave a mischievous smile.

"Don't tell me the great Mary McDermott actually lied?"

"Mary Shepherd, thank you very much."

"Don't tell me she lied?"

"Of course not." She laced her arms through mine. "I just expressed myself a bit louder than is my custom."

FIFTEEN

"Wow . . ." Mary's voice was soft and filled with wonder as she stared out the window of the plane. "Look at that."

I leaned past her and saw the moon, three-quarter's full, reflecting off the wispy clouds below us, making them glow.

"It's like a fairy tale," she said. "Oh, and look up there, do you see it? That star everyone's talking about. The supernova or whatever it's called."

I craned my neck until I saw it, a single star, sharper, brighter than all the others.

"Isn't that something? It's like a diamond, just hanging there all by itself. Have you ever seen anything more beautiful?"

I agreed and sat back in my seat. But the truth is, I lied. I had seen something more beautiful. And she was sitting right there beside me. A little girl, face pressed to the window, lost in awe. What was it about her? A naïve innocence? Vulnerability? Yes. And no. She wasn't weak. There was a strength and resolve about her I'd seen a hundred times. No, it was an indefinable mixture of opposites—fragile tenderness, compassion . . . and a steel-hard core of commitment.

Still gazing out the window, she reached back until her hand found mine. I looked down at the two of them. Hers, small and soft, willing to be wrapped inside mine, big and clumsy. I'm no poet, but even I didn't miss the symbolism. Another mixture of opposites. And beauty.

As I watched her, something she'd said back at the ticket counter still played in my head:

"You have a responsibility to love. If you do that, God will take care of the rest."

Could it really be that simple? With all the religions, all the books and philosophies . . . did it really just come down to that? I had no idea. But I did know that's what made her so remarkable. So . . . childlike. Not childish. And definitely not ignorant. But . . . unencumbered by the world. Not simple, anything but that. Sometimes she was so complicated I had no idea where she was. But it was that childlike trust that made her . . . well, the closest word I could come up with was . . . pure.

Maybe that's why God chose her.

Suddenly I wanted to pull her into me. To possess that purity, to drink it in. Keep it all to myself. But, of course, that wasn't possible. Not now. Was I jealous? Of God? I suppose I was. At least resentful that we had to share her. I smiled quietly. On the other hand, it was nice to know me and the Almighty had similar tastes.

The ticket agent had been right. We did wind up with table cloths, and as Mary had pointed out, a spectacular view.

"Roses in December," she said just a few minutes later as we toasted with our sparkling apple juice in fancy wine glasses.

"I'm sorry?" I said.

"When God takes you through winter, He always finds a way to give you a rose."

"He does, does He?"

"Of course. Sometimes you have to look for it, sometimes real hard. But if you're willing to see it, you will." Then, with an eye roll, she added, "Now if you'll excuse me, I have to use the bathroom . . . again."

I helped her into the aisle, watching her duck-foot towards the restroom. A rose in December. What a gift to be able to see things through those eyes. And what a gift to be with someone who could.

Unfortunately, there were no roses when we got to San Jose International Airport. We'd arrived just a little before two in the morning. Bone tired and, at least for me, a little punch drunk. I couldn't remember the last time I'd slept. It didn't help when I saw Mary go through another contraction. She was pretty good at hiding them but I was getting better at seeing them.

"You sure you're going to be okay?" I'd asked as we waited for our backpacks to show up at baggage claim.

"We got another seven weeks, babe." She patted my hand. "Relax, everything's going to be fine."

Maybe. But neither of us was prepared for the surprise at the car rental desk when the clerk, barely out of puberty, handed back my credit card. "Sorry," he said, "do you have another?"

"Another?"

"Card."

"What?" I asked. "Why?"

"You're maxed out."

"No way. I've barely used it except . . ." and then it hit me, ". . . except for two first class tickets from Portland."

The kid grinned. "That'll do it. What else you got?"

"I . . ." I rifled through my billfold, stalling for time to think, since I knew I only had one.

"Here."

I looked up to see Mary pulling a card from her wallet.

"What are you doing, you can't do that," I said.

"Why not?"

"Because . . . this is my trip, we're doing this for me."

She handed the card to the clerk. "We're married now. Or did you already forget?"

"But—"

"Men," she sighed. "Two days and you've already forgotten the date. Can't wait to hear your excuse next year."

"This is my expense."

She nodded. "And what's mine is yours." With a grin she added, "And what's yours is mine—don't forget that, bub."

I turned to the clerk. "She married me for my money."

"Except . . ." the clerk said.

We both waited.

"We don't accept debit cards."

"You don't accept. . ."

He shrugged sympathetically. "Sorry. Do you have something else?"

I traded looks with Mary.

"But. . ." she said, "that's supposed to be as good as cash."

"Almost."

"Almost?" I said.

He nodded.

I wracked my brain, searching for a solution. Then I had it. "But if we went to an ATM and brought you cash, you'd accept that."

The kid agreed. "Absolutely."

"Do you know where the nearest—"

"Back over in Departures."

"Great." I turned to Mary and motioned to a nearby bench. "Stay here, I'll grab the cash and be right back."

"Sounds good," she said.

I took the card but only managed a couple steps before the kid called out, "Of course you'll need a second piece of ID."

"Like my driver's license," Mary said and started digging into her billfold.

"Actually, no. We need something with a more recent date. You know, to show proof of current residency."

"Current residency?" I said.

"Like a cable bill or a utility bill or—"

"You're kidding me."

He shrugged. "It stinks, but they don't want folks driving off and disappearing with $30,000 cars."

"Right." I nodded. "I get it."

"I'm really sorry."

"It's not your fault," Mary said.

I was stumped. "So now what?" I turned to Mary. "Another rose?"

"Maybe. I'm not sure." She tried resisting a yawn but failed.

"Tired?"

"Nothing a week's sleep won't cure."

If I was tired I knew she was exhausted. "I'll call a shuttle to one of the hotels." I threw a look to the clerk. "*They'll* take a debit card."

He nodded. "Except. . ."

"Except what?"

"All the hotels with airport shuttles around here, they're pretty expensive. The cheaper ones are farther in town."

"We'll take what we can get."

"Hold on." The kid picked up the phone. "I'll ask our shuttle guy to take you."

"I'm sorry?"

He explained, "Not much business this time of night and it's only a few miles out of his way." Before I could ask, he answered, "No charge."

As he began speaking into the phone, I heard Mary give a loud sniff. I turned to see her nose in the air.

"Are you all right?"

She nodded and gave another sniff.

"What are you doing?"

"Do you smell something? I thought I smelled something. Like flowers. Don't you smell that?"

I saw her trying not to smile. Then I understood. "You mean like . . . roses?"

"Oh, right. Roses. That's what I smell." She gave another sniff.

I gave her a look.

"I love that smell. Don't you?"

I'd not give her the satisfaction of an answer—though I couldn't resist the temptation of leaning down and gently kissing her on the forehead.

SIXTEEN

Nice thing about these older cars," Mary said as she leaned her head on my shoulder, "they still have bench seats."

I motioned to the dashboard. "And the radio works. Mostly."

"I didn't know so many Mexican songs used accordions."

"Sure you can't get another station?"

She punched the buttons, worked the dial. Everything was frozen.

"You know you can turn it off," I said.

She smiled and leaned back in the seat. "Think of it as a cultural education."

"Right," I sighed.

We'd just turned onto the 101 and were heading southeast. Fresno was two and a half hours away—Charlie's place an hour and some change after that. It was barely after eleven in the morning. Even with the short winter day we'd make it before nightfall.

The clerk at the car rental had been true to his word. The shuttle driver picked us up and found us a good, cheap hotel. Well, cheap anyway. Which was okay for us. All we needed was a place to crash for a few hours.

"As long as we're bigger than the cockroaches," Mary had joked.

And she got her wish . . . for the most part.

After waking and forcing down what the hotel lobby swore was coffee, we checked the internet for used car lots. It was Mary's idea and it was a good one. If we couldn't rent a car, we'd buy one.

So, we'd hit the nearest ATM, called Uber for a ride, and ninety minutes later we were the proud owners of an ancient (Mary called it 'vintage'), turn of the century, Chevy Impala.

"Just right for starting a family," the semi-toothed dealer had insisted as I signed the papers.

It wasn't much on gas and by the faint, blue haze I saw when starting it up in the lot, I figured it was equally bad on oil. But the tires were good and for $570 it was a deal.

"See," Mary said, running her hand over the sun-cracked dashboard as I helped her into the front seat. "We're already a two-car family."

"I don't think it can handle the drive home."

"So we'll sell it back to the nice man when we leave."

"I doubt he'll take it."

"There's always the Smithsonian." She gave a slight gasp and I saw her wince at the beginning of another contraction.

"They're getting worse," I said. "And coming faster."

"Relax." She breathed deeply, blowing through it. "We've got over a month to go."

"You sure?"

"You worry too much."

"Everyone has a gift."

Once we were out of the city, we drove through gentle, rolling hills. The good news was the accordions had faded into static. The bad news was they were suddenly replaced by rap.

I sighed wearily and Mary gave me a look.

"I know, I know," I said. "More culture."

She reached over and snapped it off.

"What? So now you've got taste?"

"I've got something better." She pulled out her phone. "I've got i-Tunes." She turned it on. Or at least tried.

"What's up?" I asked

"It's dead."

"You charged it," I said. "Last night. You plugged it into the same bathroom outlet I did."

She tried again with similar results.

"Here." I pulled out my phone and handed it to her.

She took it, then looked up. "4%."

"4%?"

"Guess that particular outlet took the day off."

I gave another sigh. "We get what we paid for."

The two and a half hour drive turned to three, then three and a quarter. I'd obviously forgotten the number of rest stops we'd have to make. Like so many times before, we talked about the future . . . where we'd live, the type of apartment, how Dad would get me a job back at the mill. But most of all we talked about the baby. Where he'd go to school, how we'd save for college. And, yes, how exactly do you raise God's Son?

We also talked about the angel's message: "God will give him the throne of his father David."

"Seriously," I said. "How can we have a king when we live in a democracy?"

"How do you have a baby when you've never had sex?

"Touché," I said.

"Of course, if he's a king with a throne and a palace and everything, maybe we won't have to look for a place."

"You think he'll let us live with him?" I asked.

"Of course."

"You sound so sure."

"I'll be a mom. I'll know how to guilt him."

"Not exactly your style."

"It's genetic. I'll get the hang of it."

About the time we hit Fresno, the rain had started to fall. We pulled into a Denny's for an early dinner. I felt bad putting down the Swiss steak, fries and cherry cobbler. But not bad enough to join Mary with her Cheerios and Rice Chex—her staple the last few weeks thanks to the acid reflux.

"Don't mind me," she said, as they brought out a second helping of cobbler.

I nodded, then added, "Sure, you don't want to share?"

She cut me a look.

I chuckled as I dug in. "There's an old proverb," I said. "When God created woman, he created the fairest, most beautiful, most lovely of all creation . . . thank God I'm a man."

That earned me a pretty good punch to the shoulder.

Since neither of our phones had juice, I found an old pay phone across the street at a gas station. There, in the driving rain, I gave Charlie's mom a call, letting her know we'd be there soon.

"Oh, thank God, thank God," she said.

I could hear it in her voice but asked anyway. "Is he getting worse?"

"It'll just be getting dark when you get here. I'll fix up the guest room so you can spend the night."

"No, that's okay, we don't want to be a—"

"No, no it's not a bother. He'd want that."

"Are you sure?"

"Yes, yes, of course. Let me give you directions. Do you have a pen?"

"Go ahead, I've got a pretty good memory."

"Well, okay, then."

And that's when things started to go sideways . . .

SEVENTEEN

Babe!"

"I know, I know," I said as we inched through another deserted crossroad. I leaned on the dash, squinting passed the wipers into the dark. "There should be signs. Why aren't there signs?" We'd been traveling, going on two and a half hours, now. Mary's water had broken a little earlier. We didn't panic, but knew it best to retrace our steps back to Fresno. But things looked different in the dark, not to mention the pounding rain. I wasn't lost, but not exactly sure where we were, either.

"Joey. I need out!"

"What?"

"Now! Stop the car, let me out."

"It's pitch black out there. And the rain—"

"Now. Now!" There was an urgency in her voice, a panic I'd never heard before.

"Alright, alright." I pulled to the edge of the road, a

steep gravel embankment. I hadn't even stopped before she had the door open and was scrambling out.

"Mary!" I shoved the car into Park and threw open my door. "Mary!" I raced around the headlights and down the embankment. She was where I found her in the grass . . . on all fours.

I kneeled to join her. "What's going on?"

"No!" she shouted, deep and guttural. "Stay away!"

"But—"

"Don't touch me!" It was part-cry, part-growl as she tossed her head like a wild animal.

"Are you, is it time?"

She let go a stifled cry. Tried swallowing it back, but couldn't.

"Mary!"

Another cry. So eerie, it gave me chills.

"We've got to get back to Fresno!" I reached for her. "A hospital!"

"No!"

"What do you mean, no? Here, let me help—"

She slapped my hands away, arms flying, landing punches wherever she could.

"Mary!"

"No! No!

"Don't be crazy. Get back in the car. Get back in the—"

"NOOO . . ." The shout took everything she had, left her panting for breath.

"Alright, alright."

"Don't make me sit, I can't sit!"

"It's raining. You can't stay out here in the rain."

"No!" She began crawling away."

"Alright, alright. Tell me what to do. What am I supposed—"

"I don't—" She swallowed back the pain, forced it out in breaths. I wanted to hold her, to somehow absorb it, but she would have none of it.

"Six weeks," I said, repeating what I'd said when her water first broke. "He's not supposed to come for another six weeks."

She answered between pants. "You . . . tell him . . . that . . ."

"You can't do it here, not on the side of the road."

"You . . . tell . . ." She dropped her head, fell to her forearms, shouted and groaned.

I rose to my feet, searched for any signs of civilization—homes, barns, anything. Nothing except an old shed, forty, fifty yards off to the side, barely visible in the edge of my headlights.

"Can you stand?"

"I'm not getting back in the car. I . . . can't."

"No, no, I get that." I dropped back down into her line of vision. Her hair was soaked, face dripping. Her mouth hung open as if in a drugged stupor. "Mary look at me."

She turned away.

"No, me. Look at me." I scrambled around until I was back in her sight. "I'm here, focus on me." She tried looking away again. "No, me. Me. I'm here for you. Just look at me. Mary. . ."

Her eyes shifted to mine, dazed, barely comprehending. I spoke slow and clear. "There's a shed, just over there. It's not good to be outside like this. We have to get out of the rain."

If she understood, she didn't show it.

"Can you stand?"

She continued to stare.

"I'm going to help you stand. We'll stand and I'll help you walk to the shed. Okay?"

She closed her eyes, gave the faintest nod.

"Great." I reached for her hands and she panicked again, slapping them away.

"It's okay, it's alright. We're not getting back into the car. I promise. We're just going to walk over to that shed, get you out of the rain."

I reached out again. This time she let me take her hands. They were cold and wet. And they were trembling.

"Alright now, I'm going to help you to your feet, okay? Just keep your eyes on me and I'll help you stand."

Together, we got her back onto her feet—weak but standing.

"Good, good. Now we're going to walk over to the shed."

She nodded.

I remembered the moments after Charlie got hit—me on my knees, reciting our training. I did it with Mary. "Let it wash over you. Don't fight the pain, let it pass through. Focus on me. Let it pass through."

She swallowed, nodded.

"Good girl. Alright, then. Just walk with me. I'll take a step and you take it with me. Okay?"

Another nod.

"Here we go." I took a half step backwards toward the shed, gently pulling on her to follow. She did. I took another step and she followed. And another. She started to look down. "No, no, no. Keep your eyes on me. I'll get you there, but you got to trust me. Okay? Trust me."

She nodded and we started again. "That's it, good, good."

We were half way there when another contraction hit. She pulled away, doubling over. I tried hanging on but she fought me. "No . . . No!

I let go, gently easing her back to her hands and knees.

She groaned, swallowed another cry.

"Let it go," I said, "let it go."

But she wouldn't. Too stubborn, too modest, or both.

I waited, nearly a minute.

Then, shaking, but with raw determination, she willed herself to rise. Once up, we resumed walking, eyes locked onto one another, step after step, like some slow, primeval dance.

We arrived at the wooden shed. I pushed against the door with my back, grateful that after a slight catch, it creaked opened. There was no missing the scurry of what had to be rats. I caught the sweet smell of rotting hay and a sickly trace of old urine—again, probably the rats. The unpainted planks that made up the walls were weathered with just enough cracks between them to let in the faint glow of my headlights. The shed would do nothing to keep out the cold, but it would definitely keep us dry and safe from any wild animals in the area.

I found a corner with relatively clean hay. After stomping around it to scare off any vermin, I tried easing Mary down onto her back.

"No," she groaned, "not my back."

Before I could stop her, she rolled onto all fours and then began rocking back and forth.

"Hang on," I said. "Let me go back and grab you some dry clothes."

She gave no answer. When I was sure she was safe, I ran back through the rain to the car. I stepped over the growing stream of muddy water at the base of the embankment and scrambled up to the car. I opened the door and reached over the front seat to grab our backpacks. Hers weighed a ton. Mine, half that. I dragged them to the front, climbed out, threw one over each shoulder, and kicked the door shut. I'd barely slid down the embankment before, and I know this sounds crazy, but I swore I heard voices. Almost like singing. I turned, looked around, but figured it was a trick of the wind and rain.

I waded back through the wet grass and entered the shed. Mary was still on her hands and knees.

"Alright," I said, dropping the backpacks to the floor. "Let's see what we have." I dug through hers until I found a couple sweaters and a pair of jeans. "Here we go."

But when I brought them to her and kneeled down she pulled away. "No . . ."

"You've got to stay warm," I said. "Your dress is soaked and—"

"No . . ." she growled.

I watched, helpless and unnerved. As a soldier I was trained to evaluate, take charge, rectify. But this . . . watching the love of my life crawl on her hands and knees, suffering like some wounded animal.

Another thirty seconds passed. When the contraction ended she was shivering harder.

An idea struck me. If she wouldn't change clothes, I could at least build a fire. There was plenty of straw for kindling. I could punch a hole in the roof for ventilation. But start it with what? I had no matches, no lighter, nothing that could— Yes, I did have a lighter, in the car. I grabbed a handful of hay and after more stomping to scare away the rats, I raced back into the rain.

I found the lighter and with dripping hands pushed it into its receptacle. It took forever to pop back out but when it did the coil glowed red and hot. I placed the ends of three or four pieces of straw against it, noticing how my fingers shook. The straw began to smoke then catch fire.

But how to carry it back in the rain? I scanned the car, searching, until I spotted the ashtray. I yanked it out, reignited the straw, and carefully dropped in more bits and pieces to feed the flame. Then, shielding it with my hand, I stepped back out into the rain, slid down the embankment, and was half way to the shed when I heard her scream:

"Joey! JOEY!"

EIGHTEEN

I burst through the door. Mary had moved to the far wall. She was no longer on all fours, but squatting.

I raced to her. "What are you—"

"I have to . . . push."

I kicked aside the hay to lay down the burning ashtray. I kneeled and took her shoulders. "Here, I'll help you lie—"

"No!"

"Mary—"

"This way . . . I'm okay. . ."

"Don't be crazy. Here, let me—"

"This way." She took a breath, then another. "YouTube."

"What? I don't— You saw this on YouTube?"

She nodded through a grimace.

"You saw someone give birth like this on YouTube?"

She gasped. "Lots . . ."

"What do I do? Tell me what—"

"Hold me. Something's happening. I have to push."

I nodded. But before joining her, I grabbed both of her sweaters and draped them over her for warmth. Then I slipped between her and the wall, sitting with my legs spread so she could lean against me for balance.

Another contraction hit. I felt it through her whole body. She groaned and pushed. I wrapped my arms around her, placing my hands on her belly. I couldn't tell if she appreciated the contact, but I did. Somehow it helped me experience, though just a fraction, of what she was going through. The contraction continued. She stopped pushing, panted, then pushed again.

When it had passed she lay her head against my chest, exhausted. "I don't . . . I don't know if I can. . ."

I wiped the sweaty hair from her face and whispered into her ear. "You're doing great. Hang in there, you're doing great."

She nodded.

Then, unable to leave well enough alone, I added, "You sure you don't want to lie on your back. I bet it's a lot more—"

"Stop," she gasped.

"I just—"

"People do this."

"Right, of course," I said, silently wishing for something more medically certified than YouTube.

We stayed that way through six more contractions—Mary pushing whenever she had the strength—me, never so helpless in my life.

"He's coming!" Mary dropped her head to look. "He's coming, he's crowning!"

I followed her gaze and saw what looked like a little, black yarmulke—the top of a tiny head, wet and covered with hair.

Another contraction. More pushing.

I couldn't look away. I'd never seen anything so strange and . . . miraculous.

She paused, gasping, resting, until another contraction hit and then more pushing. The head slowly appeared, more and more black hair. Then the neck.

"Do you see him?" Mary cried.

"Yes." I choked out the words. "Yes, I see him."

"Catch him!"

"Wha—"

She clutched my hand, pulled it under her.

Another push. The shoulders appeared, followed by the rest of the body, quickly slipping out, dropping into my hands. Dropping into *our* hands.

I was stunned. Unbelievable. In that single moment the two of us held a brand new life, an entirely different life. No words could describe it. Suddenly, we were no longer two, but three. The shock and euphoria was overwhelming.

We cleared his mouth and he began to cry. That's when I noticed his coloring. "He's blue," I said. Which was a lie. He was practically purple. "Mary, he's—"

"Dry him." She pulled away the sweaters. "Put him on my tummy."

I reached over, grabbed a shirt from my backpack and dried him. When I'd finished, I laid him on her stomach. She stared at him, mesmerized.

The cord," I said. "It's still—" But I saw no need to bother her. I reached into my pocket for my Swiss Army knife. I took the umbilical cord in one hand and sawed back and forth with the other. It was tough and fibrous but easy to cut through. Meanwhile, Mary had begun covering the baby with the sweaters.

The placenta came quick and sudden. I pushed it aside and replaced it with clean, dry straw. I bunched up hay behind her so she could lean back. Her neck and shoulders were damp with sweat and coated in fine dust from the straw. I also noticed several tiny welts. Flea bites. I saw a couple on my own hand. And the baby? I could only imagine how they'd be attracted to his soft, tender skin.

"More clothes," Mary said. "We need to keep him warm."

I dug into our packs, pulled out jeans, shirts, underwear, anything I could find. Together we piled them on top and around the baby. But even as we worked, Mary, like me, couldn't keep her eyes off him.

"Have you ever seen anything more beautiful?" she whispered.

I nodded. Once we'd finished, I scooted beside them and she laid her head on my shoulder. Now it's true, 'beautiful' may not have been the description I'd have chosen. He still looked a bit alien to me and definitely the worse for wear. But, 'miraculous,' now that was a word I could get behind. And 'astonishing.' Yes. Miraculous, astonishing and . . . miraculous.

But not just him. I wrapped an arm around my wife. "You did it," I said. "You did it."

She looked at me, totally exhausted. Yet, somehow, she managed to smile . . . and I thought my heart would burst. There would be other concerns, other worries, and they'd come soon enough. But for now, we just sat there. Enjoying the moment. Trying to comprehend what all had happened.

I felt Mary adjust the child, bringing him higher to nurse as she softly spoke to him. "There you go, little one. Everything's going to be alright. Yes, we're going to be just fine."

And I believed her. We both believed her.

> "She will give birth to a son and you are to give him the name Jesus because he will save his people from their sins."

> He will be great and will be called
> the Son of the Most High.

None of us knew what that meant or what would follow. But for this moment, in this time, we would rest. As we did, I thought of Mary's words:

"You have a responsibility to love. If you do that, God will take care of the rest."

I turned to her. Her eyes were closed but she was smiling. I leaned over and gently kissed her cheek.

She found my hand and squeezed it.

NINETEEN

Twenty minutes later I headed back into the rain to turn off the headlights and save the battery. I could have left the car running to keep it charged, but like I said, the Impala was old school which meant it preferred chugging, not sipping, gas. I also decided to rekindle my ashtray and use it as nightlight. No need to build a fire. Mary assured me, at least for now, that the baby was warm. As soon as both had rested I'd get them back into the car, heater running full blast, and head to a Fresno hospital. She questioned going to a hospital since all the heavy labor (pun intended) was done. But she knew I wouldn't budge on that and finally agreed. At least that was our plan.

But as we kept learning over and over again, our plans are not necessarily God's.

I was kneeling in the front seat, relighting some hay with the lighter, when I saw the headlights in the mirror. I had pulled quite a ways off the road so they didn't have to slow. But they did.

Of course my training kicked in. I had no idea what they were up to and I had a wife and kid to protect. I checked the back seat, looking for anything to use as a weapon. Everything was in the shed. I reached to the glove compartment, smacked it a couple times until it opened. There was nothing but a sales slip, misfolded maps, a couple McDonald's wrappers, and, wait—there, an ice scraper. Cheap plastic, nothing fancy, but in the right hands the serrated edge was sharp enough to do some damage.

The car, a Toyota pickup with camper shell, pulled up behind me and stopped. I gripped the scraper and stepped out to meet them. The driver, pudgy and middle aged, opened the door. He would be no problem. The dome light showed two other men in baseball caps, much younger. They might be.

"Amigo!" The driver climbed out of the pickup. "Amigo, my friend." He shielded his eyes from the rain. "Are you the one with the baby?"

I blinked, caught off guard. But prepared myself as he approached.

"Are you the one with the baby?"

"What?"

He continued toward me, motioned to the shed. "A baby. Do you have a baby in there?"

"A baby? What makes you think—"

"The angels. They said a baby. Here. Somewhere here."

"Angels?"

"Sí, sí. A baby. In a shed. Dressed in many clothes." He turned to the building. "Is that the place?"

I've got a pretty good poker face, but he must have seen something in my eyes. Because when he stopped, five feet away, his own eyes twinkled with delight and he broke into a grin. He gave the slightest nod and I couldn't help but return it.

He turned to the pickup. "Aquíes!" he called. "Este es el lugar!"

I watched the young men pile out of the car as the driver reached out to shake my hand. "It is such a pleasure, señor." I didn't offer him mine, it was too soon, things were too crazy. But it didn't curb his enthusiasm. "You are a blessed man. Very, very blessed."

Keeping my eyes on the approaching men, I shifted my weight, preparing, just in case.

As they arrived, the driver said something else to them in Spanish and their faces lit up. Like the old man, they reached out their hands, anxious for me to shake them. I hesitated, but they were so excited and insistent that I finally agreed, discretely slipping the scraper to my other hand. One after another they pumped my hand, as enthusiastic as their leader. There were plenty of grins to go around and exchanges I didn't understand as they stood in the rain, excited as school kids, casting looks to the shed.

Finally, the driver spoke. "Señor, if it is not too much trouble, if it is possible, may we see the child?"

"You want to see him?"

"Sí, sí."

"The baby."

All three nodded.

By nature I'm a suspicious man. You never get burned by expecting the worst. But somehow. . . Maybe it was all my time with Mary, her trust, her compassion. Or maybe it was the baby. Regardless, as I searched their faces, I saw no malice. Only joy. And hope. I looked over to the shed, then back to them as they eagerly waited.

"I don't know," I said. "He's resting now with his mother."

"But the angels," the old man said, "they told us to come. We will make very little noise, I give you my word."

"Right, right," I nodded, "the angels."

"Sí."

Three weeks ago I would have written them off as nut jobs. But now. . . "The angels," I repeated, "they told you to come here."

"Sí, sí. To find a baby wrapped in many clothes."

It was a risky choice, more foolish than wise. But they seemed so genuine. And there were all the coincidences. And "the angels." Against my better judgement, I gave a nod. They practically leaped in excitement.

"But only if you're quiet," I said. "Only if you promise to let them rest."

The driver turned to the men and explained. They nodded enthusiastically.

"Okay then." I turned toward the shed. "But just for a moment."

"Sí, sí, only a moment."

We slid down the embankment and jumped the growing rivulet along its base. They turned on their cellphone flashlights as we waded through the wet grass. I switched the ice scraper back to my right hand.

As we approached the door, I called out, "Mary? Babe, are you decent?"

Her weary voice answered, "What?"

"Are you covered up?" I motioned the men to a stop. "Are you decent?"

"What? Yes, why?"

I wasn't sure how to answer.

"Joey?"

"Looks like we've got company."

TWENTY

I pushed opened the door and caught movement in the shadows as Mary pulled herself together. I signaled the men to stay outside while I entered.

"What's going on?" she asked

"Visitors. They say they saw angels."

"Angels?"

"That's what they say. Told them to come see the baby."

She continued gathering herself. "Angels?"

"They said they were to come here and see a child wrap in lots of clothes."

"Angels?"

"So they say."

Once she'd gotten herself in order, she took a deep breath, then gave a nod.

I motioned them inside. I was careful to stay between them and Mary, and I made sure they moved to the far wall, a good fifteen feet away.

They obeyed and took their places silently, reverently. Mary raised a hand, shielding her eyes from their cell lights, which they quickly lowered. The driver motioned them to remove their hats. They did, all the time keeping their eyes to the ground.

Mary and I saw the gestures and both relaxed. Slightly.

Finally, Mary asked, her voice thick and husky, "You saw angels?"

The driver nodded.

"What did, what did they say?"

The men exchanged looks. The driver cleared his throat. "We . . . work in some of the fields around here. And a camper, we have a camper we sleep in at night. To save money." He looked back to the floor.

"Tell us about the angels," I said.

He looked up, cleared his throat again. "At first we thought," he motioned to the youngest, "Edmund here, he thought they were flying saucers."

The men chuckled softly. The youngest smiled, shook his head good naturedly.

The driver continued. "They were bright, very, very bright."

"'They?" I said. "How many?"

"One at first. Floating high above us. And big. Ten, maybe fifteen feet tall." He looked to the other men who nodded in agreement. "And then he said, the angel said, I will translate it: "'You are not to be afraid.'"

"Afraid?" I repeated.

The driver explained. "We were so scared, we were climbing over each other to get back into the truck. But the angel, he said, "'Pay attention, this is very important. I'm bringing you good news, something that will give you much, much joy. And not just you. The joy, it will be for everyone.'"

"Joy," I repeated.

"Sí."

The other two nodded.

He continued, "'Because today, the savior of the whole world, he is being born. The Messiah, the great leader you have all been waiting for.'"

I cut a look to Mary. She was taking it all in, listening intently.

"And we, all three of us, we didn't know what to think. Maybe it was some kind of trick—like on those TV shows where they fool people." The men softly murmured in agreement.

"And then the angel, he says he'll give us a sign to prove it. He says we will find the baby, in a shack, a shed, and he will be wrapped in many, many clothes."

The old guy fell silent. He glanced to the floor, then back up. By now all three had worked up the courage to look at Mary. There was no missing their awe.

Mary looked over to me and I knew what she was thinking. It wasn't my first choice, but I knew there was no stopping that sensitive heart. I turned to the men and motioned them forward. "Come."

They hesitated.

"It's alright. Come closer."

The younger ones turned to the driver for permission. He nodded and they took a tentative step forward.

I motioned them closer. "Come."

I could hear Mary pull some clothes aside as they shuffled forward. They were careful to keep their lights pointed at the ground, but the reflected glow was enough. They arrived, not six feet away, as Mary revealed the baby.

They stood in rapt silence . . . until the driver slowly lowered to his knees. The other two followed.

Mary and I could only trade looks.

The driver continued. Apparently there was more to

the story. "As we stood there, listening, the whole sky, it lit up. Suddenly there were hundreds of them. Thousands. They were everywhere."

"Angels?" I said. "Thousands of angels?"

"Sí. And they were all singing. But music like I have never heard. Some, their voices were so high. Others very, very low. We heard them with our ears, but we also felt them, inside." He tapped his chest. "In here, we heard them in here." He glanced to the other two who nodded.

"Were there words?" I said. "Could you make out what they were singing?"

He raised his head and closed his eyes. "'Gloria a Dios. Glory to God in the highest. And on the earth, peace to all those who please Him.'"

He said nothing more.

The room filled with silence. Absolute, holy silence.

TWENTY-ONE

I looked to Mary lying beside me in the pickup. "You comfortable?"

No answer. Who could blame her. She was entranced by the baby in her arms.

"Mary?"

She turned to me.

"Everything okay?"

The driver hit another rut, jostling us back and forth. She nodded. "What about you?"

"Sure," I said.

It was a lie and she smiled, making it clear she knew.

I turned and looked out the tiny window of the camper shell. This was tougher than I'd thought. Not the ride, not the pregnancy, not even the birth. It was the letting go. Eight weeks ago I had a dozen men in my charge. Whether they lived or died was up to me. I'd made one mistake and as a result a man my age was fighting for his life. I'd vowed never to make that mistake again, never to let go. But now . . . now God seemed set on making me break that promise . . . multiple times over.

An hour earlier, when we were back at the shed, I'd noticed Mary's exhaustion was quickly setting in. I explained to our visitors that mother and baby needed their rest so I could move them to the hospital as soon as possible. They understood. After thanking me again and again, they headed back to their truck, anxious to tell everyone what they'd seen.

But I'd barely shut the door and joined Mary before the old man was knocking again. "Señor. I am sorry to bother you."

I grunted, got to my feet, and crossed to open the door.

He held one of the guy's cellphone lights. There was no missing the concern on his face. "I have some news that is not so good about your car."

"My car?" I stepped out and looked across the field to the road. I saw one of the cellphone lights moving about, but not much more. "What's wrong?"

"It is better if you look." He motioned me to follow.

I called back to Mary. "I'll just be a minute, there's something I've got to see."

She agreed. But before I even shut the door, the old man grabbed my arm. "Shh…" He was shining his light into the tall grass to our left. "Do you see it?" he whispered.

I squinted. "See what?"

"There. The eyes."

I spotted them, not ten yards away, glowing eerily red in the cellphone's light.

"A bobcat?" I said. "Is it a—"

The old man threw up his arms and leaped into the air. "Go! Vete! Lárgate de aquí!"

The glow disappeared into the faint rustling of grass.

"A bobcat?" I repeated. "Cougar?"

He kept his eyes on the grass. "In this area, I have never seen one. They are much higher in the mountains, not so low."

"Coyote?"

He shook his head. "I do not know, but perhaps, it is only a guess, but . . ."

"But what?"

He turned to me, lowered his voice. "El Diablo."

I frowned.

"The Devil."

I gave a scornful chuckle.

He didn't smile. "If the angels, if they know of such things . . . then why would not the devil?" I searched his face. He was dead serious. Then, with a shrug, he motioned me toward the road. "Come. Your car."

I pulled the shed door closed, giving it an extra tug, and followed him along the path we'd been making in the wet grass. Moments later I saw the problem. Instead of sitting level on the road embankment, my car was tilted at a good 40, maybe 50 degrees.

"What on earth. . ."

As we got closer, I saw the reason. The little rivulet at the base of the embankment had turned to a torrent. It had eaten away the dirt, causing the outer edge to collapse . . . the outer edge I had parked on.

Once we arrived, I jumped over the stream and scrambled up to the car.

"Be careful, amigo, the rain has made the dirt very soft."

He was right, of course. Instead of the solid ground I had parked on, the embankment had turned to soft mud and was getting softer by the minute.

"The boys," he motioned to the other two standing by the rear, "they think they can push it back up."

I had my doubts.

"And my pickup, perhaps with a rope we could—"

"No, no." I shook my head. "Too dangerous."

"Yes, I agree." He called something over to the other two who disagreed. But he made it clear the decision was made. Then, turning back to me, he said, "But your wife? Your child? How will you get them to the hospital? Señor, tell us, what may we do to help you?"

And it was that operative phrase, 'help you,' that ate at me. I should have parked better. This was my family, my responsibility. I should have been smarter, and I definitely should be able to take care of them without the help of total strangers.

I should, but apparently I couldn't. It would take at least a couple hours for a tow truck to be dispatched and come all the way out here (wherever here was). And another couple to head back No way could I subject Mary and the baby to that.

So, with no other option, I grudgingly led the men to the shed, let them load us into the back of their pickup and transport me and my family on this bone-jarring journey to the hospital. Mary certainly didn't mind. Stretching out on a queen-sized mattress was a relief. The baby didn't care. And the men were thrilled for any excuse to stay with us longer, let alone enjoy the honor of helping. Yes sir, everyone was happy. Well, almost everyone. I sighed heavily, turned onto my back and stared at the roof of the camper shell.

Ninety minutes later, far better time than I had made getting us lost, we pulled into the emergency entrance of Mercy General Hospital. The staff was good about admitting us. Well, admitting a premature baby who had been exposed to the elements. They immediately swooshed him off to their nursery. And since Mary had complained about some minor tearing, they agreed to admit her, too. It was only when we got to the paperwork that we ran into problems.

"May I see your insurance card?" the clerk behind the window asked. Her mussed hair, and sleep-deprived eyes made her look even more exhausted than she sounded.

"Pardon me?" I said.

"Your provider."

I turned to Mary. "I'm sorry, I don't—"

"You have no insurance?" the clerk said.

Mary leaned toward the window. "My parents, up in Washington, they—"

"You're 26 years or younger?

"Yes."

"And their provider?"

"I . . . I don't—"

"Can you give them a call?"

"Yes, of course." Mary reached for the phone in her backpack then stopped. "The battery's dead."

The woman said nothing.

"Can she use yours?" I asked.

She shook her head. "Hospital policy."

I frowned.

"What's wrong with yours?" the clerk asked.

"It's dead, too," I said.

She kept silent, offering no solution.

"It will only take a minute," I said. "We'll pay for any charges."

She shook her head, in no mood to help. "Sorry."

"I can't believe you'd let a little thing like—" I couldn't stop my voice from rising. "She just had a baby? Do you get that?"

"Of course I do. And County Hospital, across town, will—"

"Three hours ago she gave birth to a kid." I pointed to a window. "Out there! The least you could do is—"

"Do we have a problem?" Some tall guy in a suit appeared. They were apparently sending reinforcements.

"Yes," the clerk said. "These people have no insurance. Her parents are up in Washington and—"

"Are you the couple with the newborn?" he asked.

"Yes," I said. "And if you'd just let us—"

"Admit them," he said to the clerk.

"But they have no proof of—"

"There are some very wealthy gentlemen upstairs in the VIP room waiting for them."

"I don't understand," the clerk said.

He turned to me. "Foreign dignitaries, as best I can tell. They have agreed to pick up all your expenses."

The clerk continued to argue, "But I have to—"

"Let's get her admitted, now."

"And their coverage? There's no plan that allows total strangers to—"

"They're paying cash."

She came to a stop. She pushed up her glasses and looked up at him.

He motioned to me. "Stay here and finish the paperwork." Then to the clerk he said, "And, you, call for a wheelchair."

"But—"

"Now."

TWENTY-TWO

I didn't know they had hospital rooms like that—fancy as any expensive hotel. Leather sofa, end tables, lamps, mini kitchen, a big screen TV. And one extra addition . . . three strangers kneeling before my wife's bed.

When I finished the paperwork and joined her, I was more than a little concerned. "What's going on?" I said as I entered the room.

Mary looked up from discretely nursing the baby. "They've been like this since the nurse first brought him in."

I quickly moved between them and the bed. There was an older man, Middle Eastern looking—gray beard, dark brown jacket, brown pants. Beside him, a guy about my age in a white robe and headdress like sheik's wear. The third was some middle-aged Asian fellow in an expensive suit.

"Excuse me," I said.

At first, they didn't look up.

"Gentlemen?"

They slowly raised their heads, exchanged glances and got to their feet. The gray beard had a harder time until the sheik offered a hand.

"You're the ones who paid for the room?" I asked.

They looked to Gray Beard.

"Yes." He had a thick accent, Farsi the best I could tell.

"Why? What do you want?"

They traded more looks like it was a crazy question. Finally, he answered.

"We want nothing. But to pay honor."

"Why?"

"Because he is a king."

"*The* king," the Asian said.

All three nodded.

Gray Beard closed his eyes and quietly quoted, "For to us a child is born, to us a son is given; and the government shall be upon his shoulders, and his name shall be called Wonderful Counselor, Mighty God, Everlasting Father, Prince of Peace . . ."

The Asian added, "Of the increase of his government and of peace there is no end."

Mary quietly answered. "That's from the Bible—the prophet, Isaiah."

"Yes," Gray Beard, said. "Written many centuries ago. And there are more." As he spoke, he edged closer. "Not only from Isaiah but from many of the holy books."

The Asian joined him, motioning to the sheik. "According to Balthazar, over three hundred."

I raised my hand, signaling them to stop. "That's close enough."

"Of course," Gray Beard said. He lowered his head. "Forgive us."

I continued, not rude, but not exactly polite. "What makes you think our son, what makes you think he's this great leader?"

"The prophecies," Gray Beard repeated. "As we have said, there are over—"

"But why us, why him? How did you find us?"

"The star."

I scowled.

The Asian answered, "The supernova, it has been in the news for many months."

"And it led you here?"

"That and your government." Gray Beard lowered his voice. "They, too, are aware of the prophecies. The ones that say a king will be born."

I pretended not to understand.

He motioned to the radio on Mary's nightstand. "May I?"

I nodded, watched him carefully as he approached. He turned on the radio, found some classical station, and cranked it up nice and loud. Mary looked to me but I motioned that it was okay, I knew the drill. He thought the place was bugged.

He continued, voice barely loud enough to be heard over the music. "You have been under surveillance for many months."

"How did anyone—"

"Again, the prophecies. They say he will be born of a virgin."

"But—"

"There are not many virgin pregnancies—especially in small towns where everyone knows everyone's business."

"And have Facebook to share with the world," the Asian added.

I began to nod.

Gray Beard continued. "Because of our influence,

each in our own country, we were able to gain favor from members of your intelligence community. But you must be careful. As one would expect, not every person takes kindly to the idea of their power being usurped."

"By . . . a king," I said.

"Yes, a king. But perhaps not as they suspect. The prophecies are most difficult. Some speak of a mighty ruler. Others speak of a suffering servant."

The Asian agreed. "There are many paradoxes."

"But, as with all prophecy, they will eventually come together." Gray Beard's eyes turned back to Mary and the baby. "Into one."

The room fell silent as they all looked on.

After several moments, the Asian cleared his throat. "The gifts?"

"Ah, yes, yes." Gray Beard walked back to a leather satchel near the sofa. He unfastened it and pulled out something wrapped in blue silk. Carefully, he untied a burgundy ribbon, pulled aside the silk, and revealed a gold rod, about a meter long, covered in jewels. Big ones. Rubies, sapphires and diamonds. If they were real, it was worth a fortune.

"A scepter." He approached, smiling. "From my kingdom. It has been in my family many, many generations." Once he arrived, he held it out for me to examine. "And now it is his."

I shook my head.

He didn't understand. "I am sorry?"

"We can't take that."

"Oh, but you must. He is my king now. You must accept it."

Before I could stop him, he laid it on the bed and stepped back. He turned to the sheik. "And from Balthazar, our young friend with crazy dreams . . ." He motioned for him to approach.

The sheik was reluctant, but after another nod from

Gray Beard, he stepped forward. In his hands he held a folded sheet—blue and purple, with lots of gold embroidery. He spoke for the first time—an Arabian accent, so soft I could barely hear. "For this I must apologize. I must apologize, but I was told."

The Asian smiled. "In another one of his 'visions.'"

Gray Beard quietly chuckled. "And believe me, he has many."

The sheik ignored them and handed the sheet to me. "I was told to give you this."

I took it, not understanding.

He explained. "It is a burial shroud. From my country. A cloth to cover the dead."

I looked up. "A burial shroud?"

"I am sorry. I only obey."

I turned to Mary who looked as puzzled as me. I tried to think of something appropriate to say. "Thank you," was all that came to mind.

He nodded and stepped back.

"Perhaps," the Asian stepped forward, "you will find this a bit more appealing." He produced a square, plastic card—perfectly clear, except for nine, tiny numbers printed in black at the center.

"A credit card?" I asked.

"No. It is a code. Scan it into any digital phone. Once contact is made, enter the amount of cash you wish to withdraw, what bank it is to be delivered to, and funds will be transferred within the hour." He handed it to me. "You will find it far more convenient than cash—"

Gray Beard interrupted with a twinkle, "—and weighing far less than the gold—"

The Asian finished, "—which Balthazar, here, suggested we bring."

The sheik looked to the ground, once again embarrassed.

I shook my head. "I'm sorry." I tried handing it back to him. "This is too generous. These are all too generous. I can't accept them, let alone from total—"

"Nor do we expect *you* to accept them," the Asian said.

Gray Beard nodded. "They are not for you. They are for him." He motioned to the baby. "They are for the King."

"I get that, but—"

"Please, do not let your great pride get in the way."

"Pride?"

"We have done our research, Lieutenant Shepherd. We know of your many accomplishments and your pride . . . and your guilt. But there is a power at work here far greater than any of those."

The Asian added, "And greater than your misguided understanding of responsibility."

I blinked. There it was again. The not-so-gentle thump on the head. A reminder that I was not in charge. There was nothing I could do about my guilt over what happened to Charlie. That would haunt me the rest of my life. But my pride, my need for control . . . The orders were clear, I was to stand down.

And in case I missed the point, Gray Beard finished the lesson. "Sometimes my young friend, when the car speeds down the freeway you must learn to stay inside. If you step out, attempting to push, you will only bring pain and trouble."

I looked at the burial cloth still in my hands, then over to the sheik who had presented it. I couldn't help but think in some ways my actions would have to mirror his own. Obedience. Whether I liked it or not, whether it made sense or not, obedience would always have to come first . . . even when it made me look foolish or, worse yet, irresponsible.

TWENTY-THREE

The voice from Mary's re-charged phone rang loud and clear. "*Turn left in one-half mile.*"

Mary grinned. "Sure makes things easier, huh?"

"I could have found it."

She looked out the window, making it clear there was no need to argue—why argue when you know you're right?

I motioned to the back seat. "How's he doing?"

She turned to gaze at the baby strapped in his new car seat. "Sleeping."

"Good. Good." And it's true, everything was good. For the most part . . .

Earlier that morning, the doctor, a wise old man with thick, white hair announced there was no need to keep us around. He gave Mary a few self-dissolving stitches and, unimpressed with my choice of surgical instruments for cutting umbilical cords, a prescription for antibiotics.

"What about the baby?" I said. "A month premature?"

He shook his head. "Human gestation is anywhere from thirty-seven to forty-two weeks. He may have been a few days early, but nothing alarming."

"And the delivery?" Mary asked. "My labor, it was so short and fast."

"Without an epidural, the body sometimes works very quickly."

"That's why it was so easy," I said.

Mary cut me a withering look.

The doctor chuckled. "When the body feels pain it may decide, 'enough already' and hurry things along."

That was pretty much it from the medical department.

As far as finances, our three benefactors disappeared as quickly as they had appeared. Once the gifts had been distributed they made a hasty retreat into the early morning hours.

"Can I at least buy you guys breakfast?" I had asked.

Gray Beard shook his head. "The fewer hours we are here the less attention will be drawn to you."

"The government?" I said.

"And the food." The Asian shook his head. "We tried dinner last night. No thank you."

"When's the next flight?" I asked.

"Whenever we decide," Gray Beard said.

I nodded. "Of course. You came in on your own plane."

"*Planes*," he corrected.

After a round of handshakes and more heartfelt thanks from us, they were gone.

Then came the photos. Lots and lots of photos. With her phone recharged Mary filled its memory in minutes and begged to use mine. I agreed but insisted there be no posting. "No Facebook or whatever you guys are using," I said. "Not until we get things figured out."

She agreed but it didn't stop her from sending them to our folks. Or calling them. My parents were excited, but there was that down-home practicality: when would we be getting back, what purchases should they make in the meantime, were we sure about that tiny apartment we'd been looking at?

Her folks were much more enthusiastic, asking about weight, size, how she was feeling . . . and then, at the very end, they included one important fact.

"Hold it, Mom," Mary said, "I'm going to put you on speakerphone. Will you say that again?"

"Sure. Hi, Joseph. Congratulations."

"Thank you, Mrs. McDermott."

"Don't you think, *Annie* would be more appropriate now?"

"Right, sorry."

"I was just telling Mary, there are a couple new faces in town. Two men, very fond of dark suits and sun glasses."

I threw Mary a look.

"They even showed up at church yesterday."

"Did they say anything?" I asked. "Do anything?"

"No, no, as polite as pie. But there are those sunglasses."

Mary smiled. "Mom, just because they wear sunglasses, doesn't mean—"

"I know, I know. It was a good sermon, though. One of your father's best. I hope they got something out of it."

"So, other than the sunglasses," I said, "there really wasn't anything?"

"No, no. Just the sunglasses. And, of course, the questions."

"Questions?"

"About the two of you."

I felt my gut tighten.

"Again, all very polite, very nice—"

"What type of questions?" Mary asked.

"When was the baby due? Where did you go? When would you'd be coming back?"

"What did you tell them?"

"Not much. I mean, there were those sunglasses."

I motioned for Mary to end the call.

"What?" she mouthed.

"Now," I whispered. "End the call now."

She frowned but nodded. "I think that was the right thing, Mom. Nobody needs to know our business."

"Exactly. Now, when will you be back?"

"In the next day or so. We're just leaving to visit Joey's friend."

I motioned for her to hurry.

She gave another nod. "We'll call back a little later, okay?"

"Okay, dear. Your father says, hello. Oh, and send more pictures."

"Will do. I love you. I love you both."

"We love you, too. Can't wait to see that baby."

"Bye."

"Bye-bye. Bye, Joseph."

"Bye," I said, a bit too abruptly as I motioned for Mary to hang up. I was probably a little paranoid. And naive. I mean if three foreigners could find us, anyone in the intelligence community could. But still . . .

Once we had finished packing we headed to the lobby where, to our surprise, our Spanish-speaking friends had spent the night.

"Just in case the tow truck cannot find your car," the old man had said.

I nodded but suspected it had more to do with

spending extra time with Mary and the baby.

Anyway, we found our car and, with the help of a tow truck, pulled it to safety. After a hefty fee to the barrel-chested driver, and his insightful advice to, "Be more careful, dude, you got a kid now," we began the last leg of our journey.

Thirty minutes later we pulled into the dirt lane leading to Charlie's mom's house. Once we arrived, we were greeted by two very loud, and very oversized dogs.

"Dumb! Dumber!" Charlie's mom called as she stepped out onto the porch. She was a plump woman in a yellow printed housedress. "Get back here. Now!" The dogs settled as she headed out to join us. "Joey, is that you?"

I rolled down the window. "Mrs. Riordan."

"Don't worry none about the dogs, they won't hurt nobody."

I nodded, but waited until she arrived before getting out of the car.

We'd never met, but she threw her arms around me like family. "Thank you so much for coming. It means so much to him."

"Of course," I said, "of course. Sorry we're late. We had some car trouble."

"Among other things," Mary said as she climbed out her own side and reached back for the baby.

As to be expected, Mrs. Riordan made plenty of fuss over him—so, cute, so adorable, so this, so that. All true, of course. "And what's his name?" she asked.

"Jesus," Mary said. It was the first time we'd said his name publically. It felt good, and strange and strong. "His name is Jesus."

"Hello, Jesus." Despite sharing our joy, there was a sadness in her eyes that crept into her voice. "May I . . . would it be alright if I held him?"

"Of course."

I'd have expected Mary to be more reluctant, but she must have sensed something because she handed him to her without question. Mrs. Riordan took him into her arms. You could tell she was deeply moved—adjusting his hair, his clothes. I watched as her eyes brimmed with moisture. Mary looked on, equally as affected.

After a long, respectful moment, I cleared my throat and asked, "How's Charlie?"

She looked up, eyes glistening. "Still hanging on. I don't know how he's doing it, but he's still hanging on." Taking a breath for resolve, she passed the baby back to Mary and motioned us to follow. "Come. We'll get your things later."

We entered the house through the kitchen. It was warm and filled with the smell of pot roast and simmering green beans with bacon. We stepped into the darkened hallway, lined with family photos. Charlie's room was at the far end. As we walked, my mind again replayed the events of so few weeks ago . . .

"Joey! Look out!"

I'd been kneeling beside a seven-year-old girl on the floor. She'd been caught in our crossfire and was bleeding out. I'd broken protocol. Instead of checking the rest of the house first, I let my emotions get in the way. An unknown child was dying. Just another casualty of war. But I let the sight throw me, distract me. I was the one distracted and Charlie was the one who paid the price.

He spotted the shooter a moment before me and leaped between us. He managed to bring him down, but not before taking the rounds that should have been mine.

And, now, for my mistake, he was dying.

"Sweetheart?" Mrs. Riordan called. "Charlie? They're here."

We stepped into the small room. He lay on a twin

bed, motionless, skinnier than I remembered. Bandages still covered part of his face and his eyes were closed. I've smelled death before and the room was full of it.

"Sweetheart?" Mrs. Riordan said.

He gave no response.

I approached the bed. Mary stayed at my side. The baby squirmed but didn't fuss.

"Hey partner," I said. "You look like crap."

If he heard, he didn't show it.

I felt my throat tighten, a knot of emotions—grief, anger, guilt. Mary sensed what I was going through and rested her hand on my shoulder. I kept my face turned so she wouldn't see the tears.

I swallowed, forced out the words. "I'm sorry . . . so sorry . . ."

At first there was no response. And then he spoke. A halting, breathy whisper. "He's . . . here . . ."

I leaned closer. "Yes, buddy, I'm here." My voice clogged with emotion. "We took the scenic route, but I'm right here."

I could see it took effort, but ever so slightly he shook his head.

It broke my heart and I answered in a ragged whisper. "I know . . . if there was any way to change places with you, I—"

"Not . . . you."

I stopped. Frowned. "No, it's me," I said. "It's Joey. I'm right here."

His lips parted. I dropped my head closer to his mouth.

"No . . ." he whispered.

I looked to Mary, to Mrs. Riordan, at a loss for words. The baby began to fuss. Mary rocked him in her arms, but he wouldn't stop. She was about to turn, preparing to leave, when Charlie spoke again.

"*He's* the one . . ."

The baby grew louder.

Charlie began to smile. It was faint, but unmistakable. "*Him* . . ."

None of us understood.

The baby began to cry.

"Yes. . ." Charlie's voice was more air than sound. He struggled for another breath.

Mary's hand tightened on my shoulder as he spoke again.

"*Him* . . ."

It made no sense but he seemed determined to make his point. He fought for another breath--gasping, uneven. "Yes . . ."

And then he relaxed, letting the rest of it go in a quiet, rattling wheeze.

We waited. But it was over. We all knew it. He was gone. Only his smile remained . . . as Jesus' cry grew louder.

TWENTY-FOUR

Everything ready?"

"All set."

"Backpacks?"

"Check."

"Diapers?"

"Check."

"Baby?"

Mary looked up from strapping him into the baby seat. "Oh wait, I knew I forgot something."

I was standing next to Mrs. Riordan at the driver's side of our newly acquired Range Rover. "You know," I said to her, "I'm still not feeling good about this."

"What, the car?"

"It's worth fifty times the Impala," I said.

"You saw the letter. Charlie wanted you to have it."

"You also said those last few days he was pretty out of it."

"On this he was clear. Very clear. Besides," she

chuckled as she threw a look to our old car tucked away inside her barn. "I'm getting a collector's item, right?"

I sighed and nodded. It's true, I wasn't thrilled about the car trade, but if the letter was to be trusted, or honored as a last request, it had to be made. Actually it wasn't a letter, just a single sentence he'd dictated to his mom for us:

"Take the Range Rover so you're not tracked."

That was it. Nothing else. Except for the map. Something he'd drawn his last few weeks. Despite the shaky lines, it clearly detailed what minor road and off-road routes we should take . . . on our trip to Mexico.

That's right, Mexico.

Normally, I'd have chalked it up to a failing mind that was shutting down. Except for the dream. The one I had our second night there. The one I had just a few hours before Mrs. Riordan handed me the envelope with the note and map. This time there were no clown cars, no pies in the face, and no angels. Yet, it was just as real and just as vivid.

Me, Mary and the baby were walking around a bunch of pyramids. Only they weren't like the ones in Egypt. They were more the type in Mexico. And as we're walking, we're listening to a radio broadcast. Something about a virus hitting Fresno and wiping out hundreds of babies born around the same time as our son. It was some new and unheard of thing and, of course, the conspiracy nuts claimed it was all manmade. Whatever. The whole dream was pretty strange. And stranger still, was the man suddenly walking beside me saying, "Pay attention to this, Joseph. Pay attention."

Coincidence? The note, the map, the dream? Maybe. But I had my doubts. Especially with all that had been happening. Either way, I figured it wouldn't hurt to do a quick, sight-seeing trip down south.

Now, as we climbed into the Range Rover, preparing for the journey, I could see Mrs. Riordan tearing up. I got back out and gave her a hug. She thanked me for the hundredth time. Not only for coming down, but for agreeing to speak at Charlie's graveside service a few hours earlier. "It really was beautiful," she said. "Just what he'd want."

"I don't know," I said as I climbed back behind the wheel.

"You spoke from your heart, that's all that counts." She leaned inside and gave me a kiss on the cheek. "You're a saint."

We shared another round of goodbyes and were finally on our way.

"Saint Joseph," Mary said as she reached across the console and took my hand. "I like that."

"Hmm," was all I could think of as we continued down the dirt lane toward the highway.

To our right, a hundred yards on top of a small knoll, was where a handful of locals, a couple relatives, and I had buried Charlie just a few hours ago. Once again my mind drifted back to how stupid I had sounded . . .

'When I look around at all your faces," I'd said, "I'm probably the least qualified to talk. I mean I only knew Charlie for, well, nothing compared to you."

I looked to Mrs. Riordan, who nodded for me to continue. I glanced at my notes as they flapped in the wind.

"I don't understand why Charlie was taken from us. I don't know many guys, actually I don't know *any,* that were as good as him. And his belief in God . . . I tell you, the guy could be a real pain."

The group chuckled.

"But it didn't stop him. I mean even when he got hit,

all he could talk about was God. 'Joey, don't forget how much He loves you. He loves you, dude. He loves you.' Maybe it was the drugs. I doubt it though. Truth is I can still hear him saying it. And a bigger truth is I need to believe it."

I looked to Mary. She rocked the baby in her arms, encouraging me to go on.

"So why would God let something like this happen if He's got all this love for us?" I shook my head. "Me and Charlie, we used to get into long debates about that. And he would always come back at me with something like, 'God gave us free will. He could have made us robots so we'd always love everyone. But that wouldn't be love. Love has to be a choice.'

"'Then I'd ask, 'So why do good people suffer?' And Charlie, he'd just say, 'Don't bother asking God why. That's way beyond your paygrade—like a little kid demanding to know how a hundred ton airplane can stay in the air . . . or how an entire human being can be formed in just nine months. Sometimes you just gotta believe in things you'll never understand.'"

I took a deep breath. I was just about done. "Charlie's questions, no matter what happened, were never about 'Why.' They were always about 'How.' *How* can I use what's happening to make me a better person? *How* can I use it to make a better world?"

I looked back to Mary. Was this what was happening to us? What the baby was all about—making us better people, making the world a better place?

"Of the increase of his government and of peace there is no end"?

I glanced back at my notes a final time. "There's not a one of us here who won't miss Charlie. I think about him every day. Charlie Riordan was a great man. And what made him great was that he had the heart of a child. A child who trusted in the love of his Father. And one who was never afraid to share that love with his friends . . . no matter the cost."

That was it. I'd made it through without choking up. Now, back in the car, knowing what I was thinking, Mary said, "You did good. I was really proud of what you said."

I nodded, then quietly added, "I just wish I believed it."

"You do. Mostly."

"I guess. But I've got a lot to learn."

"We all do, Joey." The baby began to fuss and she turned back to him. "It won't be easy, but I think we've got just the person to teach us."

I nodded and took another breath. "It's sure looking that way. And if this is only the beginning, I can't even imagine. . ." I dropped off, unsure how to finish.

"Hold it!" she cried, "stop the car!"

"What?"

"Now, stop the car."

I hit the brakes and we slid to a stop a dozen feet from the main road. "What's wrong?" I asked.

"Where's the camera?"

"It's in the back. What's going on?"

She reached to the back seat for the small digital camera, another one of Mrs. Riordan's exchanges—her cheap camera for our two cell phones which she promised to destroy. Grabbing it, Mary threw open the door and hopped outside. "Don't go away."

I watched as she ran up to the mail box where Mrs. Riordan had planted some shrubs. I eased the car forward and rolled down the window as she stooped down and began taking pictures.

"What are you doing? Mary, what—" And then I saw them. The shrubs were rose bushes. Four of them. All barren because of the winter. Nothing but dead, prickly thorns . . . except for one. And there, in full bloom, on a single stem, was a giant, red rose.

I watched silently as she continued taking photos. When she was finally done she headed back to the car. As she climbed in, neither of us said a word. There was no need—although she couldn't help but flash me a quick, mischievous grin.

I simply shook my head and pulled out onto the main road—not heading north, but turning south onto the course Charlie had mapped.

I had no idea where our journey would take us — though I suspected there would be plenty more bumps, twists and turns. But wherever we went I knew we'd been given a promise, right there in the back seat—a promise that would travel with us the whole way. I also knew we'd refer to those photos time and time again—during seasons of frustration, guilt, confusion, and, yes, even doubt. The times when life made no sense, when all we had to cling to were the promises of the baby. That's when we'd pull out the photos and remind ourselves that if we looked close enough, a loving God would always be there. When everything looked dead and hopeless, amidst the winter's thorns and briars, He would always be there to offer us a rose.

I reached out to take Mary's hand as the tires hummed, the baby rested, and we continued down whatever road lay ahead.

Soli Dio gloria

THE REAL STORY

Here are two accounts of the birth of Jesus Christ found in the Bible. The first is from Matthew:

[18] This is how Jesus the Messiah was born. His mother, Mary, was engaged to be married to Joseph. But before the marriage took place, while she was still a virgin, she became pregnant through the power of the Holy Spirit. [19] Joseph, to whom she was engaged, was a righteous man and did not want to disgrace her publicly, so he decided to break the engagement quietly.

[20] As he considered this, an angel of the Lord appeared to him in a dream. "Joseph, son of David," the angel said, "do not be afraid to take Mary as your wife. For the child within her was conceived by the Holy Spirit. [21] And she will have a son, and you are to name him Jesus,] for he will save his people from their sins."

[22] All of this occurred to fulfill the Lord's message through his prophet:

[23] "Look! The virgin will conceive a child! She will give birth to a son, and they will call him Immanuel, which means 'God is with us.'"

[24] When Joseph woke up, he did as the angel of the Lord commanded and took Mary as his wife. [25] But he did not have sexual relations with her until her son was born. And Joseph named him Jesus.

2 Jesus was born in Bethlehem in Judea, during the reign of King Herod. About that time some wise men] from eastern lands arrived in Jerusalem, asking,[2] "Where is the newborn king of the Jews? We saw his star as it rose, and we have come to worship him."

[3] King Herod was deeply disturbed when he heard this, as was everyone in Jerusalem. [4] He called a meeting of the leading priests and teachers of religious law and asked, "Where is the Messiah supposed to be born?"

[5] "In Bethlehem in Judea," they said, "for this is what the prophet wrote:

> [6] 'And you, O Bethlehem in the land of Judah, are not least among the ruling cities of Judah, for a ruler will come from you who will be the shepherd for my people Israel.'"

[7] Then Herod called for a private meeting with the wise men, and he learned from them the time when the star first appeared. [8] Then he told them, "Go to Bethlehem and search carefully for the child. And when you find him, come back and tell me so that I can go and worship him, too!"

[9] After this interview the wise men went their way. And the star they had seen in the east guided them to Bethlehem. It went ahead of them and stopped over the

place where the child was. 10 When they saw the star, they were filled with joy! 11 They entered the house and saw the child with his mother, Mary, and they bowed down and worshiped him. Then they opened their treasure chests and gave him gifts of gold, frankincense, and myrrh.

12 When it was time to leave, they returned to their own country by another route, for God had warned them in a dream not to return to Herod.

13 After the wise men were gone, an angel of the Lord appeared to Joseph in a dream. "Get up! Flee to Egypt with the child and his mother," the angel said. "Stay there until I tell you to return, because Herod is going to search for the child to kill him."

14 That night Joseph left for Egypt with the child and Mary, his mother, 15 and they stayed there until Herod's death. This fulfilled what the Lord had spoken through the prophet: "I called my Son out of Egypt."

16 Herod was furious when he realized that the wise men had outwitted him. He sent soldiers to kill all the boys in and around Bethlehem who were two years old and under, based on the wise men's report of the star's first appearance. 17 Herod's brutal action fulfilled what God had spoken through the prophet Jeremiah:

> 18 "A cry was heard in Ramah—weeping and great mourning. Rachel weeps for her children, refusing to be comforted, for they are dead."
>
> —Matthew 1:18—2:18 NIV

And here is Luke's account:

26 In the sixth month of Elizabeth's pregnancy, God sent the angel Gabriel to Nazareth, a village in Galilee, 27 to a virgin named Mary. She was engaged to

be married to a man named Joseph, a descendant of King David. [28] Gabriel appeared to her and said, "Greetings, favored woman! The Lord is with you!"

[29] Confused and disturbed, Mary tried to think what the angel could mean.[30] "Don't be afraid, Mary," the angel told her, "for you have found favor with God![31] You will conceive and give birth to a son, and you will name him Jesus. [32] He will be very great and will be called the Son of the Most High. The Lord God will give him the throne of his ancestor David. [33] And he will reign over Israel forever; his Kingdom will never end!"

[34] Mary asked the angel, "But how can this happen? I am a virgin."

[35] The angel replied, "The Holy Spirit will come upon you, and the power of the Most High will overshadow you. So the baby to be born will be holy, and he will be called the Son of God. [36] What's more, your relative Elizabeth has become pregnant in her old age! People used to say she was barren, but she has conceived a son and is now in her sixth month. [37] For the word of God will never fail."

[38] Mary responded, "I am the Lord's servant. May everything you have said about me come true." And then the angel left her.

[39] A few days later Mary hurried to the hill country of Judea, to the town [40] where Zechariah lived. She entered the house and greeted Elizabeth. [41] At the sound of Mary's greeting, Elizabeth's child leaped within her, and Elizabeth was filled with the Holy Spirit.

[42] Elizabeth gave a glad cry and exclaimed to Mary, "God has blessed you above all women, and your child is blessed. [43] Why am I so honored, that the mother of my Lord should visit me? [44] When I heard your greeting, the baby in my womb jumped for joy. [45] You are blessed because you believed that the Lord would do what he said."

[46] Mary responded,

> "Oh, how my soul praises the Lord.
> [47] How my spirit rejoices in God my Savior!
> [48] For he took notice of his lowly servant girl,
> and from now on all generations will call me blessed.
> [49] For the Mighty One is holy,
> and he has done great things for me.
> [50] He shows mercy from generation to generation
> to all who fear him.
> [51] His mighty arm has done tremendous things!
> He has scattered the proud and haughty ones.
> [52] He has brought down princes from their thrones
> and exalted the humble.
> [53] He has filled the hungry with good things
> and sent the rich away with empty hands.
> [54] He has helped his servant Israel
> and remembered to be merciful.
> [55] For he made this promise to our ancestors,
> to Abraham and his children forever."

[56] Mary stayed with Elizabeth about three months and then went back to her own home.

[57] When it was time for Elizabeth's baby to be born, she gave birth to a son. [58] And when her neighbors and

relatives heard that the Lord had been very merciful to her, everyone rejoiced with her.

[59] When the baby was eight days old, they all came for the circumcision ceremony. They wanted to name him Zechariah, after his father. [60] But Elizabeth said, "No! His name is John!"

[61] "What?" they exclaimed. "There is no one in all your family by that name." [62] So they used gestures to ask the baby's father what he wanted to name him. [63] He motioned for a writing tablet, and to everyone's surprise he wrote, "His name is John." [64] Instantly Zechariah could speak again, and he began praising God.

[65] Awe fell upon the whole neighborhood, and the news of what had happened spread throughout the Judean hills. [66] Everyone who heard about it reflected on these events and asked, "What will this child turn out to be?" For the hand of the Lord was surely upon him in a special way.

[67] Then his father, Zechariah, was filled with the Holy Spirit and gave this prophecy:

> [68] "Praise the Lord, the God of Israel, because he has visited and redeemed his people. [69] He has sent us a mighty Savior from the royal line of his servant David, [70] just as he promised through his holy prophets long ago. [71] Now we will be saved from our enemies and from all who hate us. [72] He has been merciful to our ancestors by remembering his sacred covenant— [73] the covenant he swore with an oath to our ancestor Abraham. [74] We have been rescued from our enemies so we can serve God without fear, [75] in

> holiness and righteousness for as long as we live.
>
> [76] "And you, my little son, will be called the prophet of the Most High, because you will prepare the way for the Lord. [77] You will tell his people how to find salvation through forgiveness of their sins. [78] Because of God's tender mercy, the morning light from heaven is about to break upon us, [79] to give light to those who sit in darkness and in the shadow of death, and to guide us to the path of peace."

[80] John grew up and became strong in spirit. And he lived in the wilderness until he began his public ministry to Israel.

2 At that time the Roman emperor, Augustus, decreed that a census should be taken throughout the Roman Empire. [2] (This was the first census taken when Quirinius was governor of Syria.) [3] All returned to their own ancestral towns to register for this census. [4] And because Joseph was a descendant of King David, he had to go to Bethlehem in Judea, David's ancient home. He traveled there from the village of Nazareth in Galilee. [5] He took with him Mary, to whom he was engaged, who was now expecting a child.

[6] And while they were there, the time came for her baby to be born. [7] She gave birth to her firstborn son. She wrapped him snugly in strips of cloth and laid him in a manger, because there was no lodging available for them.

[8] That night there were shepherds staying in the fields nearby, guarding their flocks of sheep. [9] Suddenly, an angel of the Lord appeared among them, and the

radiance of the Lord's glory surrounded them. They were terrified, [10] but the angel reassured them. "Don't be afraid!" he said. "I bring you good news that will bring great joy to all people. [11] The Savior—yes, the Messiah, the Lord—has been born today in Bethlehem, the city of David! [12] And you will recognize him by this sign: You will find a baby wrapped snugly in strips of cloth, lying in a manger."

[13] Suddenly, the angel was joined by a vast host of others—the armies of heaven—praising God and saying,

> [14] "Glory to God in highest heaven,
> and peace on earth to those with whom
> God is pleased."

[15] When the angels had returned to heaven, the shepherds said to each other, "Let's go to Bethlehem! Let's see this thing that has happened, which the Lord has told us about."

[16] They hurried to the village and found Mary and Joseph. And there was the baby, lying in the manger. [17] After seeing him, the shepherds told everyone what had happened and what the angel had said to them about this child. [18] All who heard the shepherds' story were astonished, [19] but Mary kept all these things in her heart and thought about them often. [20] The shepherds went back to their flocks, glorifying and praising God for all they had heard and seen. It was just as the angel had told them.

[21] Eight days later, when the baby was circumcised, he was named Jesus, the name given him by the angel even before he was conceived.

[22] Then it was time for their purification offering, as required by the law of Moses after the birth of a child; so his parents took him to Jerusalem to present him to

the Lord. [23] The law of the Lord says, "If a woman's first child is a boy, he must be dedicated to the Lord." [24] So they offered the sacrifice required in the law of the Lord—"either a pair of turtledoves or two young pigeons."

[25] At that time there was a man in Jerusalem named Simeon. He was righteous and devout and was eagerly waiting for the Messiah to come and rescue Israel. The Holy Spirit was upon him [26] and had revealed to him that he would not die until he had seen the Lord's Messiah. [27] That day the Spirit led him to the Temple. So when Mary and Joseph came to present the baby Jesus to the Lord as the law required, [28] Simeon was there. He took the child in his arms and praised God, saying,

> [29] "Sovereign Lord, now let your servant die in peace, as you have promised.
> [30] I have seen your salvation, [31]which you have prepared for all people. [32] He is a light to reveal God to the nations, and he is the glory of your people Israel!"

[33] Jesus' parents were amazed at what was being said about him. [34] Then Simeon blessed them, and he said to Mary, the baby's mother, "This child is destined to cause many in Israel to fall, and many others to rise. He has been sent as a sign from God, but many will oppose him. [35] As a result, the deepest thoughts of many hearts will be revealed. And a sword will pierce your very soul."

[36] Anna, a prophet, was also there in the Temple. She was the daughter of Phanuel from the tribe of Asher, and she was very old. Her husband died when they had

been married only seven years. [37] Then she lived as a widow to the age of eighty-four. She never left the Temple but stayed there day and night, worshiping God with fasting and prayer. [38] She came along just as Simeon was talking with Mary and Joseph, and she began praising God. She talked about the child to everyone who had been waiting expectantly for God to rescue Jerusalem.

—Luke 1:26—2:38 NIV

OTHER BOOKS BY BILL MYERS

NOVELS

Harbingers (series)
That Awkward Age
Child's Play
The Judas Gospel
The God Hater
The Voice
Angel of Wrath
The Wager
Soul Tracker
The Presence
The Seeing
The Face of God
When the Last Leaf Falls
Eli
Blood of Heaven
Threshold
Fire of Heaven

NON-FICTION

The Jesus Experience—Journey Deeper into the Heart of God
Supernatural Love
Supernatural War

CHILDREN BOOKS

Baseball for Breakfast (picture book)
The Bug Parables (picture book series)
Bloodstone Chronicles (fantasy series)

McGee and Me (book/video series)
The Incredible Worlds of Wally McDoogle (comedy series)
Bloodhounds, Inc. (mystery series)
The Elijah Project (supernatural suspense series)
Secret Agent Dingledorf and His Trusty Dog Splat (comedy series)
TJ and the Time Stumblers (comedy series)
Truth Seekers (action adventure series)

TEEN BOOKS
Forbidden Doors (supernatural suspense)
Dark Power Collection
Invisible Terror Collection
Deadly Loyalty Collection
Ancient Forces Collection

For a complete list of Bill's books or to sign up for his newsletter check out www.billmyers.com or www.facebook.com/billmyersauthor

ABOUT THE AUTHOR

Best-selling author. Award-winning filmmaker. To date, Bill Myers' books and videos have sold over eight million copies. Not bad for a man who never wanted to be a writer.

He grew up in the mountains of Washington State, eight miles from the nearest town. Even with all that solitude, he read very little as a child and got Cs and Ds in the only writing class he took at the University of Washington.

"When a girl I'd dated all through high school dumped me our first year at college, I wandered the campus night after night, until I finally told God He could have my life, I'd do whatever he wanted regardless of how strange it was."

Even though for most of his life Bill wanted to be a dentist, he kept getting the impression God wanted him to be in filmmaking. "We had quite a few arguments, but because I made that promise, I changed my major to film directing and a few months later found myself in Rome, Italy studying a subject I knew nothing about in a language I couldn't speak. Talk about feeling foolish."

Bill fell into writing when he was directing a play in Los Angeles and a producer asked him to write a television show. "I discovered the power of writing through television and movie scripts, then books." Besides his studies in film directing in Rome, Bill holds a degree in Theater Arts from the University of Washington and an honorary doctorate from the Theological Institute of

Nimes, France, where he taught.

As author/screenwriter/director his work has won over 70 national and international awards, including the C.S. Lewis Honor Award. His DVDs and books have sold eight million copies. His children's DVD and book series, McGee and Me, has sold 4.5 million copies, has won 40 Gold and Platinum awards, and has been aired on ABC as well as in 80 countries. His My Life As... book series has sold 2.1 million copies. He has written, directed, and done voice work for Focus on the Family's Adventures in Odyssey radio series and is the voice of Jesus in Zondervan's NIV Audio Bible. As an author, several of his children's book series and adult novels have made the bestseller list.

He is also managing partner of Amaris Media, International–a motion picture and media company currently developing several projects for both children and adults.

He can be reached at bill@billmyers.com.